# Memoirs of INSANITY

By

Jason Green

GINGERNUT BOOKS Ltd
www.gingernutbooks.co.uk

First Published in May 2014
By CreateSpace Independent Publishing Platform



Cataloguing in Publication Data is available from the British Library

ISBN 978-1-907939-40-2



GINGERNUT BOOKS LTD
Head Office
27 Sotheby Ave
Sutton-in-Ashfield
NG17 5JU

www.gingernutbooks.co.uk

# DEDICATION

This book is dedicated to my brother who will always be missed and to those who always have faith in me and to whom I owe so very much for supporting me through all life's adversities.

# ACKNOWLEDGMENTS

This is to acknowledge all the help I have received with this book.. Debbie my cover designer who produced the fantastic cover. Michelle Gent as Editor who finally made the release of this book possible. Also I'd like to thank any of you who read my books for making all my work worthwhile.

# Chapter One

# TRUE BEGINNINGS

I was born on May 6th in the year 1972 in what was then a small town called Reading in Berkshire, England. To a mother Linda and a father James and I had three brothers and two sisters. All but one are still living - the oldest, my brother was taken at the age of nineteen.

I am doubtful whether my father was raised by his parents to have any specific profession; but, about the time of my birth, he resorted, rather perhaps as an amusement than a business, to the occupation of mechanic.

Later in life he would turn his hobby into a thriving business that would take us from our humble beginnings and change everything.

At a very young age, my father had a developed a love of cars and engines and all things automobile. He gained a yearning to learn how they worked, the way they were put together, what broke them and what had to be done for them to be fixed. In time, he turned it into his work. He was of a very active and somewhat volatile disposition, and so frequently had partners and extra-marital affairs. As I stated, I had three brothers and two sisters but that is not entirely true. Through his affairs, both then and in later life, there are two other brothers out there and although I do know their names, I have never had contact and I doubt I would recognize them if I passed them in the street. In the early days, my mother was blind my father's indiscretions and it seemed like they were invisible to her, but in later years she would open her eyes and find it too much to bear.

My earliest memory of my childhood was being held by my mum who wore a chequered dress. I cannot remember how old she was, but I remember how young and gentle she was as she looked down on me. Those were the early days; before my younger siblings and before getting older took its toll on my parents. Those were simple days; Johnny and I just crawled and played. The highlight of the week was bath time in the old tin bath. When dad used to take it off the hook, bring it in from the kitchen and fill it from the kettle. John and I had a fantastic time splashing around while mother and father sat talking or reading. As well as most Sundays, come sun, rain or snow, we took trips to the coast where dad used to take black and white pictures with his old camera.

Then as father's worked increased and incomes improved, as with all things when prosperity happens, my parents decided to upscale so we moved. No longer the tin bath and our Sundays sitting there splashing. Instead we moved to a place with all the modern conveniences. A change that might have been an improvement in the style we lived, but in a way, it damaged the closeness we once shared.

The next child came along and I started to disappear. Then

another child and then the first girl and by that time, I was hidden in the background.

I remember when I was nine, I dislocated my hip at school and I know it seems weird but it was one of the best times of my childhood. I lay in traction in the hospital bed but mother came every day and spent hours with me. I felt so special; I never wanted it to end. Father appeared from time to time but it was me and mother and no one else in the way. After I got home, I helped mum with my baby sister and she used to sit and help me with the schoolwork that was sent home. John and the others were at school so I had her all to myself. I hated when I got better and had go back to school as it felt like I vanished from my mother's view again; all that time I had with mother, the time she had found just for me and then it was gone.

I was distinguished in my early youth, by some portion of that exquisite sensibility, soundness of understanding, and decision of character and was aged beyond my years by the age of ten. I had all but put all childish things away and saw them as not important. Toys, kids' wallpaper and the trappings of childhood were of no interest to me by that age. Rather, books and knowledge became my constant companions and a yearning to learn more about life and the world. As I stated, I gave up on childish things or as my shrink would try to explain it in later life: a social withdrawal from my age group. I found it harder to express myself to those of my own age. Instead when I had to play with them, I just made up silly word games to amuse them; making up words and trying to see who could make up the silliest.

I was not the favourite of either my father or my mother. My father was a man of an unstable disposition. He could be kindness personified and then at the slightest thing, turn to cruelty. All through those early years I had experienced his hand, belt and even a piece of wood; sometimes for as little as speaking when he was trying to watch something on TV. My mother, his wife, was a submissive and she seemed blind to his nature then but later, after the death of her oldest son, something changed in the way she saw and felt about him.

My mother totally doted upon the eldest son. Her system of parenting relative to me was to let me get on with things, to give me orders as she saw things that needed doing; mainly housework or looking after my siblings. Those early years were ones of restraint and contradiction, which, as a mere child, I soon discovered to be unreasonable because it was both inconsistent and contradictory. In the evening when both my parents were there, I was expected to sit through dinner and their mutual affection without uttering a word until I was out of their presence or until they had decided it was time for them to involve me. With my older brother, the same rules were never applied. He found the greatest of pleasure in trying to push things so I would end up the brunt of my parent's displeasure.

However, it was in that unkindness or indifference that seemed destined to help the growth of my mind. It was borne from the scorn of my mother and the blows and punishments from my father. It strengthened my resolve to learn and grow my mind so that one day I would be free of them all. No longer would I be a slave to their whims and desires; I would grow beyond them and be free of the anguish, pain and torment that they forced upon me.

The way my father was towards his family during his volatile moments was no better than the behavior you would expect to be visited upon an animal. In fact, if you did give an animal the treatment we so often received, you would end up being prosecuted with the full weight of the law. My father's anger, although he was reasonably fond of us, flared at the slightest displeasure. When he walked in from work, we would dread the look in his eyes. I knew his displeasure would be visited on me or my brother, even though my brother was the favorite child. At some point during the evening, we would feel his wrath, yet those that had caused his upset would receive understanding.

Father had a way of hurting us and never leaving a visible mark. His hand felt like iron as it hit our backsides. Father used to say 'Cry and you'll get the same again!' Tears were a weakness he would not endure in his sons. If we were lucky, we got the belt and I can tell you for a fact, although you hear some horror stories about what the belt feels like, I preferred it to his hand. After years of lifting engine blocks and repairing cars, his hand felt like it was forged as it struck our young flesh.

To the outside world my father was the perfect parent and a person to be respected and liked by all. Everyone had a good word to say about him, no one saw him as we did. However, inside the four walls of our home, we dreaded his next period of displeasure. Even my mother, who tried hard with him, was sometimes the target of his anger. He never hit her as far as we saw, but many times we watched his dinner fly to hit the wall or something was thrown to be smashed and then a day later, he would replace it with a smile and an apology. He did throw her out of the door in temper one day, but he didn't hit her. That was after they had argued and there was no resolve in sight. His worst trait was that he hated losing.

My father had the inability to see that you can't win every time; there are times when you will lose.

He just couldn't see that or concede on the points. On my back I bear the scar of the time he lost in a game to me. Well, not exactly lost but rather, he decided that no longer playing the game was a better choice.

We used to play-fight sometimes in the evening or weekends. It was harmless when I was young but as I got stronger, it became rougher - more of challenge, less of a game. I was around sixteen when we had that last play fight. I had finally started to better my father and he knew it wasn't playful banter, he wanted to prove he was the alpha. As I started to pin him, he dug his teeth into my back and tore out a chunk of flesh. He wanted to hurt me and prove his superiority over me. Shocked by that, I lost my train of thought and father managed to pin me. It was to be the last time we ever had a play-fight as when father pinned me, the pain in my back was excruciating.

"STOP!" I managed to shout and as he looked into my eyes, it seemed like color left his face and a fear washed over him. I don't know what he saw in my eyes but from that day on, he avoided any situation that meant we were at conflict. Even his harsh punishments were avoided. Instead he would look at me and decide to send me to my room or he would go for a drive. I asked myself many times what he actually saw in my eyes. Did he see the darkness that was growing deep inside my head? Whatever it was, dad decided he'd rather not risk finding out what was really there.

My mother was a proud person and expected us to keep the house nice. But from the moment us kids could pick up a dustpan, she trained us to do the chores and keep the home as she liked it. Our beds were the worst bit. It wasn't until we were bringing in our own income that we had quilts. Until then, we had blankets and sheets. My father used to drop a coin on the made bed and he expected it to bounce. All corners had to be perfect 'hospital corners'. If the coins didn't bounce or the corners were not right, our beds were tossed and we had to start again.

So in truth my mother was house proud but it was us older children who kept it that way while my mum went out and did what it was she did every day. My mother hated any mess in her house, when father came in with oil on his hands, marks were left and sinks dirtied. Luckily, most of the time, my brother and I got there first, so mother hardly ever saw the marks and dirt, it was almost always clean. However, the times we did not get there before her and she commented to him, we knew that by bedtime we would feel his displeasure for sure.

My mother, although subservient to my father, had dark secrets of her own. My father had affairs and illegitimate children, I admit, but by no means was my mother innocent of those sins either; though she was a practicing catholic and a woman of the church. She would spend hours helping the local priest or helping at the convent.

My parents had a friend called Richard and although he was like family to us all, the night he and mum was seen in the kitchen in a lovers' embrace should have told a story. Although they shrugged it off and blamed drink and lack of judgment; a mistake if you will, the truth and what they were to each other can still be seen in my youngest sister's face, the resemblance is unmistakable.

My father, to this day remains blissfully blind to the fact that when Richard and my sister are together, it is like father and daughter and when both of them stand side by side you might see it too. My sister shares Richard's features and a lot of his ways. And in later life, as my sister had her own children, Richard's features would appear to be more prominent still in them.

Those nights John and I looked after our siblings because Richard and mother had gone for a drive while father was supposedly working - I rather believe he was in a woman's embrace. Those nights she and Richard were alone, when I look at my sister, I can only guess what was really going on. For years my mother kept Richard on a string. His love held him there a captive, unable to break free until the day she cast him aside, like he was worthless rubbish and she acted like it should have never been. She does admit that back then, she did fancy him. Now she would say she did then, but now? No way.

Damaged and hurt, Richard would never find another woman's embrace. Instead, he spends his life with his family, looking after my sister and her children. A true father to her and grandfather to her children like the one we had never known. A grandfather the like of which, if she had relied on my father, they would have never known as my father never had time for his grandchildren, his own life mattered most.

Richard's family knows the truth, although my mum would deny it. Her darkest secret that one day could be her undoing. But if he is my sister's father, good on him! He has shown my sister everything we were denied and at least one of my siblings has the memories all children and young adults deserve; those of a loving father. Thanks to Richard's love for his suspected daughter, he will never let her feel alone or suffer in any way. So long as he lives, I know for sure that my sister will never want for anything and their love will endure all the trials life may throw at them.

All through my childhood years, I tried to gain my mother and father's affection and approval; gymnastics, cross country running, head librarian at school - I worked hard to gain good grades. I even helped found the school's newspaper, but nothing would gain their desperately craved approval or affection.

In later life, the certificates of my efforts did appear in the cabinet in the front room, but when asked, they denied my achievements and instead credited my older brother for them. All the effort and pain I put myself through to achieve those goals and they weren't even recognized as mine. But then what else should I have expected? As my mother once told me, of all my brothers and sisters I was the one not planned for. I was an accident of fate and birth. With a start like that, how could I have expected things to be any other way? How could I have expected to be accepted or acknowledged in anything I did or achieved?

I was suspiciousness of everyone; a feeling of being under constant surveillance by my parents. I knew they were just waiting to see me do something wrong, even though they didn't have time to actually communicate with me. I knew they were waiting for me to make one slip so they could prove themselves right, that my older brother and siblings were far superior to me.

Those early years had no doubt contributed to my love of knowledge. Toys and games that boys my age might enjoy, I held them in contempt instead of relishing them and I avoided them unless my siblings wanted to play and there was no way out. The games and toys they played with held little interest or amusement for me. I was happy when it was over. But I have to admit, card games were the highlight of my times with my siblings. Black Jack and Trumps or Crib, Penny A Point; games of the mind were also a pocket money boost through their losses.

Don't get me wrong, father might have had his flaws but at Christmas he always took us to get a tree and there were piles of presents. There were more for the oldest son, but that was way things went. The year I wanted my first computer at Christmas was the first time he actually showed interest in me. He helped me set it all up. But even in that, he had a motive. He had brought a chess game for it and wanted to try it out. But I have to admit, it was the Christmas I have the fondest memories of; me and father finally doing something together, even if I didn't get a go or look-in while he was playing. That attention was short-lived and a day later, things were back to normal and I returned to being a ghost. But once I had my computer I didn't care. He had, without thinking, given me a tool that would help me gain the knowledge I needed for later life and a career.

I did have one good friend in those early years and a friend he still is to this day. Steve was full of life as a child, he loved everything and as hard as I fought to give up on childish ways, he put more effort into making sure I enjoyed them.

Every chance we had, we got away from my parents and home. We went swimming, got to ride our bikes, went for walks. We went to the same schools and he was there, day in day out, trying to keep my spirits high. He was, and is the most patient friend anybody could want. I don't see him as much now, because with age comes different paths. I will never forget and I will always be grateful for the days we had, especially those times in the cinema on Saturday afternoons, playing the fruit machines or sat up in my room playing Lady Bug. Those are the fondest memories of my childhood and will always be treasured.

Steven was my salvation and my sanity and although I have never told him, he's the best friend anyone could want. I'm also thankful for his parents. Where my parents kept me feeling isolated, his parents listened to me and spent time with me. What was lacking at home, his family gave to me and his mum and dad became like second parents to me. They would talk and listen to me, show interest in how I was. Unlike my own natural parents, his parents were never judgmental of me and I have to admit sometimes this led me to feel jealous of what my friend had. He had and enjoyed everything I craved from a family life.

But then life doesn't promise to be fair or even right and you can't choose your family, only your friends. If you're lucky, fate gives you a friend like mine. In the darkest moments of your childhood, they manage to at least show you some light.

In later life I was to gain one other good friend. A friend I would share all my secrets, a friend who would be with me through divorces and grief. We would see each other's children grow and be there for each other through good times and bad. True, much of what is in this story he didn't know but he knows more than most and no more of a trusted friend could you ask for. But then, he wasn't only *my* friend, he was my brother's too even though my brother and I never knew we shared him as a friend.

But in my eyes he is no longer just a friend, he is family. My parents, my brothers and sisters move in their own circles but I had built my own family. Maybe he's not blood, but he's the best family you could ever want. My second son loves him like an uncle and I know if there's ever a person who would be there for my kids, it would be him. My mother and father know little about my kids and partner. Yet my friend knows them all, if not by sight, then by sharing my views and burdens. If you ask my parents about my sons' likes and dislikes or what they're in to, they would have no idea, yet my friend would most probably know it all.

Kids need an uncle they can trust and know will be there for them and he has and will always be that and I know when I meet my demise, he will be there for them long after I leave this mortal coil.

You're thinking 'two friends, is that all?' but then those like me never do have many friends. I don't know why it is that way, but it's a fact. Trust and bonding is not easy for us; also, others' understanding of the way we are is not always an easy thing.

But one thing for certain, any friends we do have, we treasure. They anchor us and keep us from the darkness and we know when the darkness gets ready to engulf us, we always have them in our lives to be a safe port where we can recover. Without them, darkness and depression is waiting to take us and eat us alive. They help us cope and understand the environment that surrounds us. In copying their emotions at certain times and for future use in times similar, they help us hide our faults, to feel those emotions or even feel pleasure. We tell them everything in our lives, not out of trust but so we can gauge their reactions and know what we should show at the right time. In a way, those friends become a substitute for our conscience and emotions; without them, we would be picked on by others and maybe despised.

Was it those early years that caused the insanity that I was later to feel and embrace, or was I just born that way? A defective mistake of my parents' lust and desire given form in my creation, or was the insanity just an illness I picked up? Was it possibly a genetic condition passed down to me by an earlier generation, a redundant gene or an accident at birth? Could it have been the convulsions I had after my first inoculations? Did they damage my brain in some way to leave me defective? Could my father's punishments or the lack of affection I received from my home-life warp my mind and cause or contribute to it?

I have asked myself those questions many times over the years. Even after all this time has passed, I have no definite answers to these questions. Is my failure to now feel all but the most basic emotions a curse or a blessing? That is something I could not tell you, but it is something I have to live with every second of every day.

# Chapter Two

# INSANITY

Most of you will know love, empathy, compassion or even guilt, but to me and those like me, those are alien concepts. Going back over my childhood, was it the feeling of the lack of those emotions that helped me to become devoid of them? Could it be the fact that my mother and father withheld them from me that caused me to have problems in feeling even the base emotions? That's something I couldn't tell you. I leave you to judge that for yourselves. They are things you take for granted, but they should never be taken for granted. If you can feel those things, you should treasure them. Without them life gets so much colder and you are thrown into a place of virtual solitude.

One sure-fire mark that a man is a child of God is love. God's children are loving children. When I was born into this world, I took on the nature of my parents. Three needs: to be wanted, to be needed, and to be loved. We talk so much about love and yet we know so little about it.

I can no longer feel this emotion so am I still a child of God and light or have I become a thing, a being of darkness?

Because it has gone, does that mean I can no longer have God's loving embrace and I will be consumed by an eternity of darkness? If I am no longer a child of God because of the loss of that emotion, then as I have asked myself many times over the years, if I am no longer a child of God then am I a child of darkness or light?

When I started embracing my true identity a little more, I realized I needed to be honest with myself. I did not know what the world truly looked like. If I didn't know who I really was, if I wasn't honest and just accepted who I was, everything I tried in life would be doomed to fail. Was I a cold and calculating monster or was I trying to think of myself better than I am? Human nature is a thing that everybody talks about but no one can define precisely.

According to what I have observed over the years, mankind is a selfish, harmful being. Man seeks only to satisfy his own needs and desires. Men are motivated solely by personal gain and their own interests. Although many claim not to possess or desire those traits, they believe themselves to be devoid of them and seek to prove it by broad-based popularity, or egotism. It is those people and their emotions which serve to strengthen the gap between my kind and theirs.

The normal man, if that is the correct term, is a being that is consumed by production and consumption; is motivated entirely by his own material gain. Mankind claims to make 'rational choice', but will always choose what benefits them, even at the expense of others. However, to those like me, their choices are not governed by the same rules. We look at things and see what needs to be and should be done. We want, we get. We need, we get. If giving to others helps to improve things, then we do it. It is not greed, but it is logical that the gains be made by those it would most benefit.

When I observe those who are willing to go out of their way for others, do they do it out of love? That seems rather a myth. Look into their actions and the selfish thoughts behind it. Most of the time selfishness can be found, even if they are unaware. They give to others yet make it known that they are the ones who give. They do a good deed or job and expect a reward for doing it. Is that not a true sign of selfishness? They give to the homeless – it's not to help the homeless for the sake of a good deed, but rather to get the homeless off the streets. They reduce the risk to themselves from these beings and make places look safer and better. Would they offer to house them, clothe or feed them? I think not. Rather they place the burden on society to solve the issue. The word 'human' is a part of 'humanity' but is there humanity in their views and actions? There is a very small group who are in some mysterious way what I would like to expect from those with emotions. They choose to risk their own survival in order to ensure the survival of others, with no explanation as to why. If they saw someone freezing, they would give them warmth in the shape of a blanket; small actions but selfless in their intent. Why few lack the selfish streak defies explanation, for even the most unlikely looking can be one of the few who will show that trait. Their kind seems to be rarer than mine who is devoid of base emotions.

It is to this kind of person we are prepared to give help and support. Not for emotion but because they are logically the way forward. They are the true humans who do show humanity. Not the monsters that society creates.

They are true humans to whom we look as friends, discarding the others of mankind as colleagues and acquaintances. If we call someone 'friend' you can be sure that they are true and selfless persons.

'Happy', 'sad' and 'normal' seemed to be the only base emotions I am not numb to and so I am able to feel them. To fit in, I learned to emulate and mimic the correct responses and at which times they should be shown. The selfish greedy ways of man just seem alien or even feared and others who feel them are the ones who are unlucky. Don't get me wrong, I think I was once like everyone else and felt things - or did I? It's just been too long to remember. Did I ever feel those things? If I did, I apologize out loud to the world at large.

One thing we do share with mankind is the ability to take life. The first life I took was a bird that had been caught by my brothers. Though parasite-infested, it was still an innocent creature. It had an injured wing and its chirping was an indication that the bird was suffering and dying slowly. As my brother went out, I went into his room and took the bird. I held it in my hands and looked at it, wondering how it could suffer so. It was so small and helpless yet that didn't distract me. The distressed chirp had to be silenced. Where was the logic in letting it suffer and die so slow? I held it in one hand then rubbed its neck gently with the other and a quick flick of the wrist and its life was ended. Finally that bird was at rest and its suffering had ended; the lifeless body an empty shell, devoid of life that I cast gently into a corner.

When my brother returned they assumed it fell out its box, got caught and died. The truth was that if he could have found a way to silence the chirping and cure the agonizing pain, the bird's life would have been spared. But then if he or my parents had really seen the suffering in the bird they wouldn't have been so selfish in thinking of their son's want, instead they would have done what was needed and what was right. To let a helpless creature suffer so when it had done no harm was wrong. To me, it was so obvious it was going to die.

It's only now, reading my diaries that the memories return and I realize how easy it had all begun. How different I was from them even at that very young age.

When I was a teenager, I loved to go away camping for a day or two. It was on those trips that many lives ended at my hands. I am allergic to fish so I had the best of excuses for hunting my food. Rabbits and game birds were my prey and I found pleasure in the hunt. Guns, knives, even bows were never my scene. I preferred the patience of snares and traps. When my prey was caught, I wouldn't allow the snare or trap to finish their life. Instead, I went in and released them and took their final breath in my own hands. Always with the satisfying snap of the neck, feeling their precious life-force drain and disperse. I had the power of God over those innocent creatures. In my hands they would live or die the choice was mine not theirs.

But I never took a life for the sake of it, the only lives I took were for food necessary to survive. Yes I did like to take life, but life was to be respected and my own set of morals and rules was made. Never the young, or the females; they were always set free without a mark on them, taking just the knowledge not to fall into another less compassionate trap that way. Guns, bows and other means meant the animal might get injured and live and spend a short life in agonizing pain. I respected my prey too much for them to suffer. Strong males were always my victims of choice and as I skinned and prepared those lifeless bodies for my consumption, I took great care to show them the respect they deserved and not let their lives be wasted.

I detest those who take an innocent creature's life for game or pleasure. All through my life, as I heard or read about creatures destroyed; wolves, foxes and other creatures,

I would think 'why couldn't these callous hunters be treated the same and let their victim's family treat them the same?' I have to admit, it's lucky I had never met any of those callous monsters, as I would have craved for them to feel some of the torment they had inflicted. Lucky for them, I never had the chance. Instead, I resort to petitions and rants. The Canis lupus is my creature of choice and one I greatly respect. And may I say if that's an emotion, it's one I can fully admire. Though a predator, it is an integral component of the ecosystems to which it typically belongs. Wolves are not monsters, they are wild animals. They are social creatures, able to develop relationships and social bonds. They do not kill for pleasure, greed or amusement, like man. Those creatures kill out of necessity, for food and defence. If necessary, they would sacrifice themselves to protect one of their own.

Not like those pathetic humans who, out of spite, greed, fear and amusement would hunt them into oblivion. Not caring how much pain they inflicted on male, female and cub. To man with all their emotions, the kill is for fun. In the mask of lies and self-justifications they hide behind they try to brand those majestic creatures as soulless monsters that should be wiped out, when in reality, man just craves their pelts. Man with all their petty emotions are the monsters; not the wolves. As I know full well, if I wasn't a chameleon and hid so well in man's society and they saw who I really am, I too would become the hunted and caged. In some situations, I too would have been hunted into oblivion just like the wolves I treasure so. Wolves have more emotions than me but in reality are we so different? Like them, I enjoy the hunt and taking the kill. Like them, it's only for food, not for pleasure. Ask yourself who would you rather be like - my kind and the wolf or the so-called 'normal humans' that hunt them? Are you not born of the true monsters in this story?

A wife or partner leaves you, it hurts, and you cry, feel upset and are prone to rages of jealousy and revenge. We just carry on as normal, 'til someone new comes along. I suppose that's why I get on with my exes; the fact that I do not hold a grudge and I do not have to place blame. Same as death, I don't miss feeling grief and I'm glad I will not feel that burden. Someone dies, I have to admit, they do leave a gap in my life but there are no tears of sorrow or even regret. At this moment, you might think 'this is garbage' or 'he's not for real' but believe me, it's true; as any like me can tell you.

In the early days, it wasn't easy. It took two marriages and untold amount of lost friends and upset family before I learned those valuable survival traits. One thing in my favour is that I do not feel anger. Don't get me wrong, I am capable of aggression to a level that most would run if ever they see it; not through anger, but as a necessity of survival.

Those who hurt what is mine might get to see it, but normally, I am easy-going and seen as harmless. You might be thinking: 'what do you mean by *what is mine*?' You would use the words 'those you love or care about' but to those like me, love and care is not an easy way to explain it. To us, those that touch us become ours and we do anything to make sure they are safe and protected. No one takes or hurts what is ours; if anyone dares, the results may not be pleasant. Sometimes it gets complicated - as with my second wife and friend - I couldn't act because I'd have lost them both, so talking seemed the logical solution and it worked.

You might be thinking: 'is he for real?' I can assure you it's as real as it gets. We don't play games and everything we do has a reason. Even writing this story is for a reason; nothing is on the spur of the moment.

Twenty four years have passed since the condition, as the doctors called it, was first detected and it was only through acceptance and support of a few good friends that I have learned to cope and live with it; even though it could have been with me far longer. I read through the diaries I have kept over the years and still no sure answer can be seen. I can see where it took hold, see its path, even see in my diaries where it got worse, but why am I this way? That's something for you to decide as I share these diaries with you.

My demons are always there in the back of my mind, fighting for control and even one momentary lapse can have them come pouring to the surface. But over the years, my mind has built its own defences from the demons that wish to engulf me. In my mind, every day of my life, a war is fought between good and evil. My only release is in my dreams. Dreams that to most would be their worst nightmares, yet to me, they are a release and a calming influence. My dreams are things out of the worst horror stories you could ever read, the most horrific horror films you could watch and in time I will write them down for my avid readers. Starting off with the least disturbing, each story will go further and deeper into the darkness that is held inside my mind.

I know I can't say anything about all my actions during the early days of my illness. If I had told the doctors, it would just have been used against me and given them reason not to let me go. These people think they have all the answers even when they don't. But no one could help or see what was hiding in the back of my mind; the headaches or the darkness that was spreading out, trying to take over. They couldn't see that a voice was calling out to me night and day. Everyone thinks they have all the answers but how can they? No one can see what's grown inside of me. Truly, in the early days, I thought suicide would be my only logical release.

In what you have read and all that will follow, be sure it comes from my diaries and is laid out for you to read. All but the most disturbing things are included but what is given to you, I think, will be disturbing enough. The last Twenty four years, from my eighteenth year would be too long to list day by day or to cram in one book so instead, I let you into the key moments. I leave it to you to judge if I should have taken the easy way out when it all began. All I ask is that you save judgment till the very last word.

# Chapter Three

# THE STORY BEGINS

Ever since I was eighteen I had felt it there. A feeling like there was someone else inside me; someone sharing my mind, sitting and waiting for the right moment to jump right out. The presence was always to the back of my mind. Whenever I tried to look for it, the presence moved. It felt as if it was a person, someone growing inside of me. I talked to her sometimes, hoping she would answer me. I didn't know it was a she for definite, but it felt like a female presence.

The first time she appeared in my mind was a day I find hard to think about. It was the first time I saw my brother after his demise. That day was also the end to my family - or rather the beginning of the end to all I had known - and it would change everyone's lives forever; casting a dark shadow that eventually would engulf us all.

The night before, my older brother had gone out and was

traveling alone on his way back from taking a friend to the hospital. When he was on a dark country road, something caused his motorbike to slide out of his control.

Brakes screeched as the bike went over, sliding across the road. John's helpless body was dragged by the weight of the bike. Road surface bit into him, grating his clothes like cheese in a grater. It must have been terrifying, the lack of control as he slid; his head rocketing towards a post. Fighting not to hit it, to change direction, but the bike's weight trapped him, taking him, like a guided missile. His head crashed into the post. In his last moments, I can only imagine the terror and fear and a moment of unbelievable pain as the post shattered the visor and crushed his face deep into his skull. As blood ran down the helmet he would have had no time for either fear or a tear. Drop by drop, his precious life's blood left his body. Beat by beat, his heart slowed. Every drop pooled on the path in a warm red puddle, till silence and an eternal sleep was all that remained. Lying on that dark road, all alone. If it wasn't for his kindness to a friend, he would have been safe at home.

I remember waking up; mum was in tears, telling me that he was gone and I remember my disbelief. Thinking over and over that it was a terrible mistake and he couldn't really be gone. I had to see for myself and prove that it wasn't him and that it was all a terrible lie.

All the way to the hospital, I kept thinking they had made a terrible mistake. Even walking through the hospital I was preparing to tell them they were wrong. But when they took me into where John was laid out, as the door opened to the chapel of rest, a twist in my guts and a cold sensation running down my spine told me they weren't wrong and to expect the worst. He was in a room on his own and I think my overriding thought was that I didn't want John to be frightened. Obviously he would've been, because it was such a terrible accident, but it was just the feeling that somebody I loved was laying there and I didn't want him to be on his own. My mother had told me about the accident and I had expected to see him damaged and unrecognizable. Looking at my brother in the white sterile room, with blankets laid over him, it looked like he was in the soundest sleep. Injuries cleaned, and apart from a slight cut on his nose, he looked like nothing had happened.

I reached over; not believing my brother was gone. But I think the overwhelming feeling was that I wanted to share. I can't say I wanted to share what he was experiencing but I wanted to be there with him so he wasn't on his own. I talked to him and I reassured him that he wasn't on his own. I got up and held his hand. What I felt sent a shiver down my spine. It was no longer the warmth of my brother; what was beneath my touch was no longer the person I grew up with and loved but an empty shell; cold and hard to the touch. That wasn't my brother. All that had made him was gone, no longer inside the body. He was just an empty husk or shell, laid where his living body should have been. His soul departed his mortal coil for a place reserved for the likes of you and him but never for me. Sadder still was the thought that he was lost to me for eternity. For even when I leave my own mortal coil, I know his path and mine will be separate. My brother had walked in the light and that would be his path for eternity. I had chosen the path of darkness and shadow and for that reason, we shall never be together.

Should I repent of my sins and all the mistakes I had made? It would have been so easy to go to confession and be absolved. I just had to walk into a Catholic church and ask for confession. I knew I could not follow the Hippocratic ways of the church. In all my reading and studies I had seen all the misery and bloodshed in the name of the church and their God. How, in good faith, could I honestly be part of that?

They preach understanding and compassion yet throughout history, it seemed it was only for those that believed. All my life I had watched as they follow the church like lambs following the shepherd. If you pointed out the truth of history, the holy wars, the missions and all the bloodshed they had wrought, the lambs would bay: “heretic”, “blasphemer” and “unbeliever”. Honestly who in a good conscience could follow their words? Better to walk an eternity alone than to plead ignorance to the facts of what they had done.

It was as I let out an ear-piercing scream that she first appeared in my mind. Tears flowed down my face and a lump the size of a golf ball appeared in my throat. They were some of the last tears of sorrow I will shed for the rest of my life. But then I ask myself this: Was she always there and did I just ignore her? Did the immense feelings just open the doorway to let her out? They are questions that I will never know the answer to.

‘This should not be him, it should be you!’ She screamed out in my mind. ‘You’re worthless and bad! This should be you not him!’ Her words repeated over and over in my mind. I was trapped, stuck to the spot. Even when someone finally came in, it was imposable to move. All I could do was look and think: ‘Why him? Why him?’ Leaving that hospital was just a blur. So many thoughts on how it happened, who was to blame. Inside me then, the darkness began to grow, festering, hurting and nobody would know.

Days passed in a blur. Every chance she had, she tortured me in my mind, telling me how the wrong person had died. Then on the day of the funeral, my brother was brought home for a few hours before taking his final journey. Laid there in his cheap wooden coffin and best suit in the front room seemed like a farce. My brother was on show to everyone, like some type of trophy.

All the fake feelings that were being shown in that room; so-called family that hardly gave him the time of day were praising him and saying how sorry they were and how much they would miss him. It was a game for them to see who could score the sympathy points. I left the room, able to stomach no more and I went and sat with my own thoughts in the kitchen, wondering how I could teach those fakers and false friends the error of their ways. On the side of the sink was a sharp knife. Not thinking, I went to reach for it. As my hand gently folded around its handle, I came to my senses. The voice inside was screaming to me: 'do it do it!' and the temptation to follow the thoughts in my head was beyond belief. It was my mother's face peering round the door that finally settled my internal fight. Seeing her tears and dismay, I knew I owed her that much. She might not have been the ideal mother, but she had raised me the best she could and lost her favourite son. If it wasn't for my mother and what I felt for my brother, that place could have been one of mutilation and massacre.

All those others were spared their fate, not because of pity or feelings towards them, but because a woman had lost her son and deserved better. For the rest of that day, there had to be a truce between what I wanted to do and what was right. An hour later, as I watched my brother being lowered into the ground, I could no longer shed a tear. Rays of sun broke through the clouds like streaks of gold. I watched the coffin finally rest at the bottom of the hole and handfuls of dirt thrown in and I heard the thud as each handful echoed on the coffin that held his remains for eternity.

Looking around, I could see the tears in man, woman and child, but deep inside me, a coldness and darkness had grown. Empathy, love, warmth had left - if ever it was truly there in the first place - and what remained were coldness and a thirst for the pain to leave. Not a tear could I shed, not a word left my lips as I stood there. One by one they left 'til I was that the last one remaining and then I said my final farewell.

'Good bye John, rest in peace,' was all that left my lips and it was over. He was officially gone.

After, we went to my parents' home. I had to politely sit through hours of their false sadness. The 'you're the oldest now' speeches that I received wore me to despair. He was barely in the ground and they were looking for me to replace him. I sat there amusing myself with the thought of what I could do with mother's sink cleaner. A few drops in a glass here and there then that travesty would grind to an end.

I sat with the last of the stragglers before silence came down and as the day faded, I told my parents to rest and I cleared all what was left of the fakers' mess. Cleaning up food off the carpet and glasses left half-filled, I started to think and wonder if the send-off was one he would have wanted and whether it had done him justice.

In the darkness, as I lay in my bed that night, I screamed at her to leave me alone but she never listened. She just kept tormenting me, trying to take hold. Memories of my brother flooded my mind; all that we had done together and everywhere we had been; all I should have said and done. The images of that box in the ground, the thought of what would be soon happening to his shell. The thought of him decaying and the worms and bugs feeding on him was too much to bear; his organic substances being broken down into their simpler forms of matter.

But it was all too futile, he was gone and I was alone. Yes I had other brothers and sisters but they were too young, not like us. We had raised each other, comforted each other through our father's wrath. We had shared our life and dreams. None of my other siblings were as we were and none could ever be.

In the darkness of night, under its blissful cover, I used to walk where risk followed; waiting for those who dared to cross my path with aggression or anger. All that I felt inside about my brother's death was released on those that would do me harm. Nose bloodied, bones damaged and things I dare not describe. I visited all the pain I could on those animals; everything that they deserved, but always I stopped before ending a life.

Some nights when I missed my brother most, I would visit were John met his demise. On that dark and desolate road, occupied by only darkness and shadows, no sound could to be heard but for the wind blowing through the leaves of the trees. Shadows moved in rhythm as the wind caught the branches far above causing them to sway. Shadows danced and played under the light as its faulty bulb flickered and glowed. In those moments, as I stood there, I would try and make sense of why he was taken so young. He was someone who never did wrong. Why someone like me would be left to walk this world and someone like him was taken. If there was a God, was this his cruel joke on me and all who cared about my brother?

Months passed slowly for all. Family and friends became strangers and drifted apart as the misery showed. My brother was so cherished and loved by my parents. The object of their affection was gone. The whole reason for their marriage and them being together was no longer there, just the void his loss left in his place. As I watched them, I saw how neither could bear to look at each, other let alone be in the same room. Mother was the first to crack. She had to blame someone and I was first to feel her grief. The words from her mouth one day: "The wrong son died." The words hit hard as they echoed the words of my inner demon. Confirming all that I prayed was not true was in fact true and a cruel joke had been played by fate.

My father changed overnight. He was no longer happy, even his aggression left him. It was like his whole body was filled with nothing but sorrow and grief. My mother, once submissive to him, turned on him. She was submissive no more. My father was the point of blame for her greatest lost. He had brought my brother his first motorbike and lighted my brother's obsession. In mother's eyes, my father's actions were to blame. All the times he showed aggression to her precious son reared its head in her mind. He had caused her precious son pain in life and his action lead to her precious son's death. He was to blame. He had brought my brother his first bike; he had supplied the tool that led to my brother's death. In her mind she reasoned him to blame and nothing could sway her from that fact to this very day.

The rot had set in and neither seemed to acknowledge my existence, let alone have time to talk. Days turned to weeks and then into months and then one day, while I was away, father packed up and left. Neither bothered to notify me or care whether I knew or not. I was away for months and not a word. Did they really care so little of my feelings and how I found out?

Drink, drugs, women; nothing seemed to help me feel. I was numb inside, fighting to feel anything. Pain was the only thing I seemed able to comprehend. The home I grew up in was becoming a shrine to my lost brother and I could no longer remain. I moved out one day; not because I was asked to, but rather I could no longer live with the ghosts that filled my home.

Living in one room, in a bedsit all alone, I resorted to all means to kill the solitude and emptiness I felt deep inside. Nothing eased the emptiness that had filled my very being. The gap my brother filled had become a void that I felt every moment. Sleep was my enemy and I tried everything to avoid it. I downed gram after gram of amphetamines. Yes it stopped sleep, but after a time, it felt like the world was even more against me. I walked down the street and it felt like I was being watched. I came to the point where I pulled a man out of his car thinking he was there to get me. Then came the night that a dead face was at my window; a white-skinned face like a mask of death. I screamed, 'You're DEAD!' but was rewarded with a smile. I hid under my covers and apart from the use of the bathroom, for days those covers were my only retreat. Food and water lost their importance.

Why had he come to haunt me? What had I done to make him come back? As the amphetamines wore off, my body failed and sent me into a deep, dreamless sleep. I don't know how long I slept but it must have been days. Exhausted and worn-out, the whole world against me, I knew it was time to leave. Every time I went out I could feel that dead face watching me. From the corner of my eye I could see him in windows or on buses - anywhere I went. Late at night as I walked, I could hear him behind me, but when I looked, he would vanish. The times I did see him standing there he would just look at me. There was never any sign of emotion on his face and he would not speak to me or even try to. As I tried to approach, the moment I blinked my eyes he would just vanish. What was he trying to tell me? What was I doing wrong, why would he never stay around and answer? It got to the point where I started to think of my death and funeral. Was life just a trick and everyone I knew had deceived me? I knew what I had seen and felt, I knew what I was. Or was I really gone and was this all real or just an illusion?

I kicked the amphetamines - or I should say my supplier cut me off. My credit line was exhausted and no matter how much I begged or pleaded, there was no way to raise money for more. I had already pawned everything I owned to fuel my need and there was nothing else left. Reluctantly, I was forced into withdrawal. But the craving was still there and the damage it had done to my body and mind were still there. And worse was to come over the next few weeks; hot and cold shivers, not being able to focus, extreme tiredness and irritability. I crawled under the sink in a ball many days. Stomach hurting, I couldn't stop throwing up; the nausea was a nightmare. Food lost its meaning; I became fearful if I ate, the nausea would get worse. I lived on juice and water when I could. My sleep was irregular and when I woke, it was in a cold sweat or a panic. The whole of my body screamed out for release; 'A few more grams please!' would run through my mind. At one point, if someone put a mountain of it in front of me, I would have gladly tried to snort the lot. But even as the withdrawal ended, the cravings were still there. Even as I think about it, I still get the odd urge to try it again. They say admitting you have a problem is the greatest obstacle. From my experience, it's not. The greatest obstacle is saying 'no' to it day by day 'til you have broken the chain in your mind and it's a chain that never seems to break. In time, the withdrawal ended, cravings did die down and the old me slowly showed through. But the cost of my addiction was clear as I looked around my room and saw that I had nothing left; barely the clothes on my back. Even looking in a mirror, I saw the ghost of myself. I was no longer the person who once I was.

On a cold winter's night, while I sat in that cold, empty room, I made that final decision. I had to get away from my life and leave everything behind. It was the only way I would make sure that I had finally broken my addiction. I phoned one of my last remaining friends to help me pack up and I moved all my belongings to his attic. I never told him about her in my mind, even though I wanted to so badly. Nor did I mention my visitor that wouldn't leave me alone. I knew he could see I was not right, but as with everyone else in my life, it was accepted as grief.

Two nights later I was in the back of my younger brother's car on the way to Dover. I lay there listening to the music and my brother and friend chatting. Life seemed so simple and normal during the hours of that journey. Slowly drifting off into deep sleep, I thought of everything that had happened and how the trip must be. I was awakened sometime later by the call of my brother to say we were there.

I have to admit that that night, I had a journey that would stay in my mind for the rest of my life; the feeling as I sat on the top deck of the ferry, listening to the sounds of the ocean and smelling the sea air, watching the lights and white cliffs fade into darkness. I was watching a scene that had taken place in my mind; going from brightness and gradually moving into darkness. Looking overboard at the sea in the darkness, the majestic beauty of it, it was all I could do not to reach up and jump over. Part of me did consider that ending, sliding overboard and sinking below the water into oblivion. Never to be found, at last at my final rest.

But sadly, that wasn't to be. For one, mothers stood by with their kids and would have called for help and the chance of being saved was way too high to try that. It would have resulted in me being locked away and that was a fate I was unwilling to bear.

At this point you may be thinking, 'is this just a story or is it truth?' well that's something only you can judge and decide on for yourself. You see, unless you know me, you will never know the answer and those that know me will never know about this story. Another solution is: you can put it all to the test but this is a dangerous option and not one I would advise.

The rest of the night went by uneventful. I went below, brought a hot drink and then returned to my perch, thinking back and about all that was behind. It was at that point I wrapped my jacket round me, settled on a seat and drifted to sleep. The next thing I knew; was I was woken by the change in the engines. I watched as the sun was rising and the ferry was slowly moving to its destination.

Standing there waiting for the ferry to slowly pull in to the docks for us to disembark, I wondered what would be ahead of me. I had never left England before and I was there alone, moving on to my destiny. As a child, I had dreamed about one day doing it, but now it was out of necessity. Alone in a world that was strange and alien to me but then the world I had left was just as strange and alien to me. Had that much really changed?

# Chapter Four

# FREEDOM

As I disembarked from the ferry I was surprised to see that before me was similar to what I had left behind. I had expected to walk out into a new world never seen before, but the roads, grass, trees looked the same. Even the birds in the sky looked the same. I walked out of the docks at last, feeling free.

But that first day in France was to become an eye opener. I left the port where I heard couples and kids chatting away in English, and I noticed the English was fading. As I walked, it was like my own language had gone and those around me were using an alien tongue I had never heard before. I could not speak a word of French and as I walked on, it was becoming like I was deaf and mute. Have you ever heard the term 'alone in a crowd'? Try going somewhere where you can't understand a word they say and you will soon realize that it is a true fact. Even ordering basic food is a challenge.

Finding your way around or even finding a public convenience, forget it. You might have thought it would have been scary, but to be honest, after all I had gone through, that level of solitude was paradise and best of all, with everything going on in my mind, she was silent and that made it all the better.

I walked around exploring Calais and it was an interesting place; so many new smells and things to see. I saw a sign that looked like a train station or rather pointed the way to one. I had yet to learn how to ask directions. As I walked into the train station, I spotted what looked like a newsagent; sadly the man didn't speak English, so I tried pointing to what I wanted then handed over a ten franc note and was given a few coins in change. To this day, I don't know if I was given the right change.

I purchased a ticket to Paris, luckily the counter lady knew English and it was easy. The trip to Paris was the start of my education into French. A student sat by me and was too eager to spark up a conversation. I admit, thinking back, I feel sorry for her. I had her spend the whole journey drumming some key words and phrases into my addled mind. Outside, the beauty of the French countryside flew past and left me speechless. I never dreamed such beauty existed. But to her credit, by the time we arrived in Paris, I could order basic food, ask the time, and ask directions. Now to you seasoned travellers and language experts, you might think that wasn't a lot, but to me at the time, it was a lifeline. It was the difference between being dumb and mute and surviving.

I had gone from deaf and dumb and made my first few steps into that untamed world. A world I would eventually grow to respect and understand.

Paris was an experience. Tourists see one side, the people who live there see another, but to those darker few, there is a side to Paris that many don't see or they care not to see.

I was to discover that by accident, but the accident lead me to delve deeper and find that Paris was a city that appealed to my inner nature. Look around Paris and you see a glittering capital of fashion, art and culture. I explored the Eiffel Tower. I couldn't possibly visit Paris without seeing the Eiffel Tower. I did not want to visit it; I could see its top from all over Paris. The great metal tower, 300 metres above Paris like a giant metal beast. The magic of the River Seine will take hold of anyone's imagination. The water is like a mirror in which the city finds its own reflection. For poets, painters, philosophers, novelists, architects, lovers, suicides, and finally, tourists, it has cast its magic upon them all. Watching all going about their passions was an amazing sight. Even the Notre-Dame in its awe-inspiring Gothic splendour was a sight to behold. The sights in Paris were too many to number. But it was beneath my very feet, in the realm of the dead, a place where thousands have found a final rest; where I would find what I needed.

Walking down those spiralling steps into a claustrophobic world where skulls greeted me on every side might sound scary or gruesome to most but it was peaceful in that realm of the dead. I felt relaxed and at peace. Thousands spending their eternity in an artistic arrangement is a fitting end to a short life, to become art for generations to remember. If I could feel sadness, it would have been the place in my life I would have felt it most. Even though peaceful, the sorrow permeated the very walls.

In that place of the dead, thousands would spend their eternity in darkness and slumber. I walked around taking in all that was in front of me. I thought I was the only one in the chamber. A quiet sigh filled my ears, echoing around the very walls. Was it a ghost or phantom? In the dark realm anything was possible to imagine.

The night in that place was chilly. I remained still, refusing to shiver. Any movement would be heard by what was waiting. I didn't want to be the prey that it stalked. Even my breathing was slow and regulated, so as not to mist in the unnaturally cold air, though my heart wanted to hammer its way out of my chest. My body wanted to fidget, every instinct telling me to move, to do something, preferably to run away, but I waited; listening, watching.

I looked for signs of where it came from, fearing that it might not be that of the living. In that place of the dead, if ghosts existed they would definitely reside there, in darkness and shadows. I kept hearing footsteps behind me. Looking back, I saw a dark shadow on the ground. As I stood there watching, I gained a new understanding of darkness. All my life I had lived in the light but my acceptance of the darkness inside became real at that point. My torch dimmed as the shadow grew. Footsteps grew closer in that realm of the dead. Images of ghost and spectres flew through my mind; what was it? Was something hunting me? Was that going to be the place I finally met my end? In that place would I spend eternity in company of the lost souls that lay here for eternity for all to see?

A bright light appeared in my field of vision and seemed to dance in the air. Coldness of the tomb sunk into my very soul as the ball of light moved closer still. Was it the dead-lights I had read about in the horror books as a child, the lights that take the living and capture their souls? As the light moved closer, a shape had started to form behind it. A figure formed and was slowly illuminated. A woman, was it a spectre or was it a ghost? As it got closer it became solid. In that place of darkness I met my sweet Catherine. Never have I found such a tormented soul as myself since. Catherine was darkness personified; pale skin, dark eyes and a look that seemed to stare into your very soul. Not spectre or ghost but warm to the touch.

The moment we stared at each other, there was a link of kindred souls. In the place of the dead I had met someone. Together we would share pleasures that defied the very gods. My sweet Catherine, even though our time together was short, we burned so bright, reaching for the stars.

We walked through the tunnels hand in hand, talking constantly, her accent lighting my very being. Up the spiral stairs then slowly back to her place in the dead of night. After the place I had been, night would never hold terrors for me again. Death and torment had followed us both; me in the loss of my brother and her in watching her parents die. She too had felt the icy shell of those she loved and not been able to reconcile the feeling of an empty shell - no life or soul, just a husk; empty and devoid of the ones she loved. The Grim Reaper had given us a unifying bond. She embraced her inner voice and accepted mine as I had. If I had known then what I know now, I would have embraced my inner voice at that moment and accepted it. But I was new and still feared my inner demons.

She had been in the realm not to explore, but rather to get away from everything and think. As she told me it was the one place in a city so full of the living where she could finally be alone to her thoughts. The darkness below held no fear for her, it was the city above that was wrong and held the danger; not from the dead but rather the living. Who cares why she was there? She was a kindred spirit.

When I entered her room and took her into love's embrace, I looked deep into those hypnotic eyes. I was hers to do as she willed. My mind was lost and those eyes went through my head over and over and over, filling my whole mind. Perfect. Perfect. You're Perfect, a beauty of darkness. While my brain continued to blow a fuse, my heart flew into a panic in my chest as my perfect sweet little Catherine took those first three steps forward and stood but an inch away from me. She raised her hand and placed a delicate finger on my shoulder, and moved it up my neck, sending shivers through my very soul, tracing it to my forehead and down my face, across my jaw to my chin, slowly dragging it down my throat, gently brushing it across my collarbone. She paused as I shuddered, the hair on the back of my neck and my arms standing on end as my breath stopped. She continued, like a spider hypnotizing its prey, watching her own hand as she moved, barely brushing the skin on my neck again before intertwining her slender fingers around my waist, pulling me so close. She slowly raised herself and stretched; moving her mouth closer to my unguarded neck. She pressed her red lips so softly and gently on my neck. I closed my eyes, inhaling sharply. Her warm breath gave me shivers once again. I felt a sharp, pleasurable pain then warmth. Looking down, I saw a drop of my life's blood on her sweet lips and a fire in her eyes that was not there before. No fear or panic came across me, just acceptance, like it was something I could not escape.

As she fed on my life's blood, a warmth and pleasure filled me like I had never felt before. I hungered to find out what it felt like to feel someone's life's essence on my lips as mine was on hers.

I had not the teeth to pierce skin and knew it would be futile to try, but as she rose, she presented her neck and shoulder to me; skin so pale, so perfect and so soft and smooth under my skin, just like a peach.

"Sorry my teeth won't," the words came out of my mouth and she reached across to a table, picked up a knife, gently drew it across her shoulder and pulled me down to it.

The first taste of blood is an experience not easily forgotten. The warmth of the blood on your lips, the pleasant taste as it fills your mouth, massaging all your taste buds in ecstasy before gently flowing down your throat is a pleasure. Filling you with warmth that can't be given justice in the way it's described.

As she returned to my blood, I tasted hers and joined in an embrace of life's essence; a unison that nothing could take away from us. Feeding and sharing our life's blood carried us both away, the very life blood of the other. Feeding with Catherine was a time I never wanted to end, yet I have never had that pleasure again.

She moved me towards her bed, undressing me as I undressed her. I wanted to speak but her finger was brushed over my lips to silence me. Slowly she manoeuvred me down onto the bed, kissing me gently. She bound a silk scarf around my eyes. In the darkness, I heard her drawer open and all kinds of thoughts ran through my head.

Catherine raised my left arm and I felt a sharp bite at the wrist. A shiver of apprehension ran down me. Then the right arm was raised and a bite at the wrist again. Coldness went through both wrists then the skin felt like it was being pulled tight. I tried to pull my arms down but it was like my own skin was holding me there. I took a steadying breath, reaching for calm. It was too late. Untold fear flared violently in the back of my brain and threatened to overpower the trust that I had so willingly given. The fear fought with the trust and they wrestled, fighting for dominance of my mind.

I tried to call out to ask what was happening, but as I went to utter the first word, Catherine's voice softly spoke out.

"Trust me," and with those gently spoken words, I lay there as both my ankles were bound. There was a sharp pain in my chest on both nipples and the chink of chain. I knew if I asked her to stop she would but curiosity drove me on, helping to overcome the fear and doubt I held deep inside. Light returned as she removed the scarf and I could see myself; bound by my very skin. Silver needles had been threaded through my skin then tied by ribbons attached to rings on the bed. The two needles through my chest were attached to golden chains but not joined to anything. Helpless, exposed, I watched as Catherine worked on me.

I was nervous, it was the first time I had been restrained, let alone had needles passed through my skin. Excitement and then the need to see where it would go drove me to want more. Catherine leaned down to kiss me; soft, gentle kisses, I returned them hesitantly.

"It will be fine," Catherine reassured me, and stroked my cheek. "It will hurt, but it will be fine." She kissed me again, a little harder. She ran her hands down over my chest, playing with my nipples, pulling at them where the needles had gone through. A shiver of pain went through me and I started becoming aroused. She moved over me, straddling me.

Her hands reached for the chains and pulled the ends down to her. I raised my head and saw two rings, one in either flap of her labia and watched her attach one chain to each. As she attached each one, I felt my nipples pulled tight. The head of my manhood was just under her, her hips lowered and the chain went tense. The feeling as I slid into her, the warmth embracing me as I slid deeper, the chains on my chest pulling tighter sent waves of pain through me mixed with pleasure and delight.

We kissed and the bed rocked with the movement; her hips swayed forward and back. Each backward movement sent waves of pain through me at first but the pain slowly stopped and it became pleasure. Straining against my bonds, I felt my own skin betray me.

I looked deep into her eyes and saw her own expression of pleasure. Violently she moved then. No longer rocking back and forth in a gentle rhythm but up and down, driving me like a jack hammer. Each time she raised and lowered sent shivers of pleasure and pain through me. As she climaxed, she tightened, causing me to pull tight against my bonds and convulse and climax like never before. Both of us staring deep into each other's eyes as wave after wave pulsed over us till finally it passed and faded.

As I softened and slipped from her body, Catherine undid the chains and gently removed the needles. She cleaned the excess blood with her lips tenderly; not wanting to waste a drop before wiping me down with antiseptic. Then she lay in my arms till we fell into the deepest sleep, our bodies drained and our inner demons quietened. I was Catherine's and would deny her nothing. All doubt and fear had been removed from me. My body and soul were hers to control.

Catherine wasn't a vampire but she embraced their love for the taste of warm human blood. Even if she was, and vampires did exist, who cares? To me she was perfect. I still carry the reminders of that first night as scars. No one has ever been told how I got them and placing my fingers over the marks, and thinking back has brought me some minor pleasure in the dark nights since.

During the next few weeks, she took me to places I never knew existed and she taught me dark pleasures that no normal person could have ever imagined. All the rules society once taught me went out of the window and my precious Catherine taught me that maybe there are no limits to what can be felt or done.

At that point you are thinking; 'Can this be true or is it all fantasy?' I can assure you Catherine is as real as you are and the marks remain on my body to remind me of our time together. You are the only ones to ever be told this part of my life and what Catherine and I did has remained between us to this day, locked in the diaries from whence this story comes. I did not share these details to shock or entertain you, but rather so you can understand the journey I had taken, how I moved away from the light and how darkness took hold inside of me. In time, I may write about everything, but a lot of what we shared was too dark even for this story. The tamest glimpses of our time are all I dare to show. Much more, and the laws of mortal men might not endure. Society's rules can bind us tighter than any chains; what's right and what seems wrong, the common person will blindly obey. But to the few like Catherine, the experiences that can be gained overrides all such laws of oppression. In those weeks together, she undid all the pre-programmed rules and oppression and freed me to experience life as in *living*. Sadly, most of you may never be free to explore. You may claim to have lived and explored, but restraint of society's view or legalities and decency actually controls your thoughts and actions. Ask yourself, have you really lived or ever felt free? Think back to earlier in my story; the blood, needles and chains and what I have told you. How your mind reacted to the thought of that. Could you or would you willing open yourself up, let fear slide aside to explore that side or would you see it as a perversion? Could you ever be that free or would you choose to live in society's prison, chained up, repressed until you grow old and meet your eternal end?

But with all things, life got in the way and we had to part. Catherine had to leave and go on tour and I was too uncertain and scared to follow. What a fool I was to let her go, but with youth comes lack of foresight and stupidity. Deep inside, part of me fought and pulled me against the idea of going.

I had sipped from the darkness and craved so much more, yet the inner voice seemed settled for then. Even though my time with Catherine had ended, my inner demons seemed to be at peace.

It was a Thursday morning when I waved goodbye to Catherine at the station. She had offered me her place till she returned, but I stupidly refused and explained I had a journey of my own. Years later I did return to find her, but where her flat once stood was just a piece of land covered in rubble.

Those days in Paris had opened my eyes and taught me so much about pleasures and desires that most would never see or feel. If it wasn't for my demons, I would never have dared to tread in those dark shadows. I had left the world of man's God and tasted the pleasures of the darker world. I wish I could have told you the rest of the dark adventure Catherine and I explored. The few pages in this book don't do it justice as the diary held ten times the details you have read. But just to put your mind at ease, I will drop a few tell-tale tid-bits in case I ever do write the full adventures we shared. Candles are not just for lighting. Graveyards are not just for the dead, they can also be a place to spice up one's dark pleasures. Feeling your hands upon the cold stone as your partner's tied to it below can bring a great excitement and although a great sin, it's an experience once tasted is never forgotten. Leaving Paris was hard and there was a deep longing in me to return, but with what was to follow, it would be a long time before I'd get the chance to tread those streets again. But never again would I taste the dark pleasures that I had so far endured. In time, others would come.

Standing there, completely alone, unsure where to go; Paris had been like a playground where I could learn and grow but I was at a crossroads. The choices were: return to England, back to the life I had once known or travel on to see what was ahead of me - the unknown.

When I left England, I had said to my friend that I would have to be on my death bed before I'd return and as I stood there at the station, those words rang in my ears. There was no way I'd return home like that, I wanted more.

When I left England, I was still a child of the light but my journey into darkness was well on its way. If there was a heaven and a hell, I knew heaven would no longer hold a place for me. For the sins I committed in that short time would deny my entry and my eternity was sealed.

Marseille in the south came into my thoughts. I don't know how or why I thought of it, but somehow it seemed right. All through the journey, I thought back to my sweet Catherine and everything we shared. I missed her and all she was to me. The train journey was long and I spent it looking out of the windows or lost in my thoughts of those times before. No longer was I lost in a strange land. I had accepted it as my own. When I arrived I was both deaf and mute but now I could speak and be understood. Yes, basic it might have been, but day by day I was learning and growing.

I arrived in Marseille early in the day. The air was filled with the smell of the sea and the aromas of the local restaurants invigorated the very air; the noise of the clientele of the busy cafes, having a good time enlivened me.

I had only arrived a few hours previous and was heading to the fort on the hill when I decided to take a turning through a tunnel cut through the hill to the other side. Dim lights illuminated the tunnel, making it possible to see only a few feet ahead. In the darkness behind me, I could hear a noise. Was it a footstep, was it breathing? I could feel my heart start to beat faster and fear gripped me.

"Is any one there?" I called, but received no reply. I speeded up my pace and the noise behind me became clear. Footsteps speeding up, heading towards me. A silver glint reflected by the dim lights of the tunnels as I looked forward, getting ready to run. Then there was a sharp pain in the back of my head, and darkness. I must have been out for some time as it was daylight when I awoke. My left arm felt numb, white specks in my vision, a sense of dizziness and nausea; my head felt like someone had inserted a white poker inside it.

Slowly I climbed to my feet, tired and disoriented; numbness in the left side of my body. On the floor where my head had lain was a pool of drying blood. I checked my pockets and my wallet was gone. On the floor in front of me, I saw it. All the cards were there but the ten franc note I had drawn from the cash point the night before was gone. As I checked my pockets again, I realized my passport was gone too.

I couldn't believe it. Someone had done that to me for just ten francs and a passport. Was my life worth so little to others that they would try to end it for such a small amount? An overwhelming desire to be home took over. There was a bit of cardboard lying near the entrance to the tunnel which I picked up. I didn't have a pen and there was no one nearby to ask, so I re-entered the tunnel to where the blood was drying and used it to write on the card the word 'England'.

By then the pain had become unbearable and I found it hard to concentrate. The only thought in my head was that I must get home. My feet felt like lead weights and I do not know how I managed to will my body on. Much of the next day is a dream-memory in my mind and from time to time events come back. I remember standing by the autoroute - what we would call motorway - with my sign. I remember a truck driver pulling up. I remember the look on his face, the colour drained from it. Then he asked over and over: "Are you alright?"

"Please get me home." Seemed to be only words I could utter.

"No problem mate, I'm just on my way back to England," he replied and virtually dragged me up into the cab. I remember him taking a pillow and a travel blanket from the sleeping area behind. When he placed the pillow behind my head, I heard him gasp. Everything went dark again and it was some time before I awoke. Next to me I found a bottle of water.

"We'll be back in England in couple of hours. I couldn't find your passport for the docks, have you got it?" he asked.

"They took it," I mumbled through my dry lips

"Don't worry, I'll get you through," he replied, opening the bottle and giving me a few sips

For hours I lay there, drifting in and out of consciousness. The smell of truck fuel and music from the radio comforted me as pain wracked my broken body.

When we got to the dock at Calais, he handed over paperwork to a man in a uniform and the man pointed to me. The truck driver just said: "Driver's mate," and it was left at that. Twenty minutes later, we were on the ferry home. When we arrived in England, the driver kindly detoured and drove me to Reading even though it was hours off his route. To this day, I wish he had told me who he was so I could have done something to repay the kindness he had showed me.

I was dropped outside A&E at the Royal Berkshire Hospital

"Why have you dropped me here? I want to go home" I said.

"You need help mate, and I'm sorry, but I'm not taking you any further," he replied.

Grudgingly, I walked forward. As I looked back, taillights of his truck faded into the distance.

Thanks to the greed of another, I was home in England. Ahead of me, the entrance to A&E got closer and closer. It was like I was in a dream world. Everyone around me were mere shadows. As I opened the doors, my legs turned to jelly. The world started to swim then darkness engulfed me.

Gradually the darkness faded away from my eyes and

everything slowly came back into focus. My head felt fuzzy and the pain that I once felt from my head had seemed to die down. Around me, I could see beds and people moving around. Everyone was bustling about and from nowhere appeared a ginger haired woman; a woman with eyes that a man could just fall into. As I looked into those eyes, it felt like I was drowning in them. She gave a little smile and for a moment everything seemed to vanish; the pain, what had happened, even where I was.

"You back with us then?" she said.

"I'm not sure yet, it feels like I've done ten rounds with Giant Haystacks," I replied.

She went and fetched a doctor.

My doctor was a nice enough chap. He must been in his early forties. He prodded and poked me, asked a load of questions; some I couldn't answer. How could I tell him the reason I was in that area of France or what I had been doing? I would have other questions asked and most probably be committed for the drinking of blood, alone let alone the voices.

I spent many weeks in the hospital while the outer signs of my injuries healed. My skull repaired and the bruising died down, but the nightmares of that day wouldn't go. Every night, in my dreams that day played back in slow motion and I would wake with sheets soaked from my sweat, my heart racing and a feeling of terror and helplessness. The headaches grew worse as the doctors cut down my pain relief because the break in my skull had healed.

As I lay there day after day, I thought back to my sweet Catherine, wishing that she was there, turning my pain to pleasure in her own sweet way. All the darkness we had shared, no pain she ever inflicted on me ever felt bad.

Every headache was like a searing white hot poker had been pushed into my skull. I was brought up to never cry, but that pain was beyond endurance. Each time, tears streamed down my face. The codeine phosphate they gave me took the edge off, but nothing stopped it completely. The MRI showed scarring to the frontal lobe of my brain and I was told I might have the headaches for a long time to come, if they stopped at all.

Worst was to come after I left the hospital, I faced a battle I might not win. The time had come when she was no longer just a voice. It was a time when she started to take over. I felt like I was dreaming, or more specifically, that I was half-awake, a passenger of my own mind and incapable of pulling myself back to reality. When interacting with others, it felt as though they were on the other side of an invisible barrier or pane of glass.

I would scream 'help me' but they never heard. I could not connect with them though I could hear, see, feel and understand what they were doing and saying. To them, I appeared to be perfectly fine and normal of course but it was she who was the person they were interacting with; I had no control.

It felt as though I was pulled back into my mind and she was driving. My body and my skin was no longer my own. When touching something, I could feel it but at the same time, it was like I wasn't touching it.

I tried to believe those feelings weren't real, that the voice didn't exist and it was all a bad dream, but the harder I fought the sensations and feelings, the stronger they became. To the point where I hardly felt myself anymore, she was taking over day by day, I was losing what little remained. She was becoming me and I was dying slowly, trapped inside my own mind, suffocating like a voice buried in darkness.

I tried to force the voice away, to try and push her out of my mind. The more I wanted that voice to go away and the more I tried to forcefully separate it from my being, the stronger it became.

It must end, it must be over, I could bear the torment no longer. She must go, even if it was to mean my end as well; better to die free than to live a life as a prisoner in my own mind. It wasn't life and it wasn't living, it was an existence in a new form of darkness; a darkness of another's making.

Sitting there in there, in the darkness of my mind, I could hear her calling out to me. Tormenting me, telling me she would be better left in control and how I was worthless and had no right to exist. She could make better use of what I was; better than I ever could.

How could she be so cruel? I did nothing to deserve that treatment. I never did anything to deserve it. Better to sleep an eternal sleep than put up with the misery any longer.

I hate sleep, I can't sleep, I must sleep, but I must live. There wasn't enough time for anything anymore! I found myself going through each day trying to do a little of everything and by dusk, I had accomplished nothing. She took over and burned my precious time away. My life, my dreams; nothing worked out. I needed a day that lasted longer, one that never ended, never interrupted by sleep. I didn't know; I was so lost. I just didn't know what to do. I hated the standoff, the not knowing what she was going to do next. The thing was, I always felt alone. Sometimes I found it so hard to go on each day.

One night during a period of my control, I felt so alone lost and tormented. I reached out and lifted the bottle of vodka and heard her scream 'NO!' As I took the first gulp, my other hand reached to the bottle of pills in front of me. I put them to my lips and took a deep swallow, nearly choking as the pills flowed down my throat. A few gulps of the vodka and dizziness started to set in, and then cold as I was engulfed by the darkness, drifting into what I hoped was final, peaceful oblivion.

Suddenly I was jerked back from the darkness. Bright light filled my vision.

"Open your mouth!" came from a voice somewhere near.

I felt something sliding down my throat, scraping the tender flesh. I fought the feeling of wanting to choke on it as I felt it slide down into my stomach. The feeling of my stomach being ripped out followed as my stomach was emptied of the remaining pills.

"WHY?" I cried out weakly as tears rolled down my face. "Why did you do this to me?" I was frustrated and confused then darkness returned.

Gradually the darkness faded away from my eyes and slowly everything came back into focus. Around me, I could see beds and people moving around. Everyone was bustling about. From nowhere, appeared the ginger haired woman.

When I looked round, I saw a mirror attached to the wall by the sink near my bed. Looking into the mirror, I could see black around my mouth. My teeth were black from the stuff the hospital gave me to neutralize the pills I had taken.

Felling humiliated I cried to myself; 'Wake up, wake up, you're dreaming!' But it wasn't a dream. And my nightmare was not going to end.

I was no longer the person I had once been. All vestiges of normal emotion - if I ever had any - finally left my being and what remained was coldness. Tears and sorrow, happiness and guilt had left me. What remnants of what I had been was gone and what was left was all I could be.

As I lay there, a very slim and well-mannered lady from social services came to visit me at my bed. She asked a few questions, such as why I'd done it, would I do it again; how I felt. I tried to laugh it off as a drunken accident. But nothing I said seemed to get her to believe that.

I unknowingly had entered a new realm of law: involuntary commitment. I had crossed a line, demonstrated in concrete terms that I had become a danger to myself and others. I needed evaluation by a mental health professional to determine whether I had to be involuntarily committed to a mental hospital.

"I think its best we send you somewhere to get the help you need."

My first instinct was to run. I really hated the idea of being committed but I already knew if I ran it would be so much worse. I had a friend who was committed once and he ended up being taken by police in cuffs after being sedated once they caught him. If I was going to face it, I would face it on my own terms.

I sat there on my bed thinking of all the ways to get out of this while they arranged the transport to the mental hospital and time dragged on. Thinking I'd go there and be out in a day, all I had to do was act calm and hide what was inside. I didn't realize how obvious it was to others that I had a problem and try as I might, it was one thing I could never hide.

# Chapter Five

# ASYLUM

I was wheeled to the ambulance in a hospital chair that was raised and pushed into the ambulance. A nurse accompanied me on the journey. Chatting all the way, I was grateful for her company even though I hardly heard a word. I knew they had me and there would be no escape. If I tried, it would confirm their thoughts. My only hope was to let it play out.

When it finally came to a halt, I was lifted out of the ambulance. I looked around and saw that I was heading towards an old building. It had the look of an eighteenth-century Gothic building with massive grounds.

"Don't worry we'll soon have you settled in," the nurse near my chair said. Large wooden doors opened and I was wheeled in. In the distance I heard the doors behind me shut and lock. I was wheeled through a maze of corridors and eventually pushed through another large wooden door. As we entered, I heard the turn of a key in a lock.

To me, the image of an asylum was one that held crazies trying to break out; dark twisted places with staff who were cold and heartless. That was the image of the places I was brought up to believe through television and books. Maybe when the asylum opened one hundred and thirty three years before, it might have been like the horror stories. But honestly, to my surprise, the place that looked like a haunted mansion from the outside, was warm and inviting inside and the staff they were kindness personified. Inside, in some places, it still had a very Victorian look although as I was wheeled through, I never saw chains or strait jackets. Although I did hear there were strait jackets if needed.

Actual psychiatric wards are not like they appear in the movies. Your roommate doesn't look like a movie star, nor is there some comical person trying to lead all the others into mischief. There is a distance kept, an invisible wall used as a divider among the patients.

Some patients who were forced to be there believed they weren't crazy or insane and that everyone else was. Then there were those who knew they were crazy and wanted you to be part of the gang. Sometimes, whether you liked it or not, they insisted you join them.

But then there were the depression patients and the anxiety cases or day patients who could leave anytime they wanted. They talked openly and to some extent, made the first days bearable, updating me on what to expect.

That first night was an experience! The ward held both male and female patients, but at either end of the wards. There were other doors that led to rooms that actually looked like hospital wards. Those would be where we slept; one door was for the males the other as far away as they could get was the females sleeping area.

In films they mostly portray sleeping rooms in asylums as rooms with one or two beds, with big metal doors that close and lock, but in reality that was far from the case. In that place, the sleeping areas looked like normal wards. The only thing that was the same as the films is med times; standing by the window, waiting for meds; not that I wanted them. But as I was warned by another patient barely five minutes after getting there, don't try to fight taking your meds because you could get meds the easy way or the hard way and on that first night, I didn't fancy the hard way.

Ironically the patients seemed saner than some 'normal' folks I had met on the outside. Normal persons were greedy, selfish and uncaring but inside those walls, I found nothing but friendship and kindness to a level I had never known before.

On the web and on television, you hear all the stories about how mental patients are treated in those places. Well I can tell you as a fact, most of those stories are wrong. The stories of staff standing around ignoring patients, of patients being left to rot - from firsthand experience, I can tell you they are all untrue

The truth is the staff members in those places care deeply and do involve themselves. I saw staff doing jigsaw puzzles with patients, sitting talking to others, even trying to get some to play games. If a patient looked bothered or upset, the staff went out of their way to help the patients. This is fact not fiction, anyone who says otherwise has not been a patient or must have been in a place far different to the place I was in. You do get the patient who, after being locked up, has a grudge and to those I say: 'Remember what really happened, not what your anger blinds you to'.

Another myth is that you are locked up on ward, day in, day out. The worst patients are, but even then, if the staff can find a way to take them for a walk around the grounds, they will.

I had to have two members of staff with me at first, when I wanted to leave the ward. I think it was for others' safety more than my own, or maybe it was just they thought maybe I would do a runner. One day I did, but I'll get to that later in the story.

That first night in the asylum was not an ideal experience. I was half expecting to not wake up or even worse, wake up at the mercy of another patient. I did not spend too much time with other patients that night, instead I chose to go to the sleeping area, pull my curtain round and get into my bed. I should have waited till night meds were given but being my first night, I didn't know any of the rules.

I got changed into the starched hospital bed clothes and lay there listening to the world beyond those curtains; not knowing what to expect. Minutes turned to hours and silence remained. Then I must have drifted off. As darkness fell, the night nurse had woken me to check I was ok and give me my sleeping meds. I gave her a funny look; why wake me for sleeping meds when I was already asleep? But then what was I to know?

I was awoken at seven in the morning by the patient in the next bed, arguing. At first, I thought it was a nurse, but as I laid there and listened, I recognized the type of argument he was having. It was one I have had so many times over the years. He was arguing with his inner demons as I sometimes argued with mine. It actually relaxed me to know that someone else was similar to me; a kindred spirit in this prison that society had made for us. Watching the sun gradually peep through the windows, I first got a decent sight of the sleeping area. When I had come in the night before, the lights were on low as it was late, and not much was visible, but in the early morning light, I could see it looked just like a normal hospital ward.

From my bed, I reached over and drew the curtains back and saw others stir. In the morning light, you wouldn't have thought any of us were sick nor had the problems society had branded us with. We were all just patients in a hospital ward, waking to start our day. First thing to go through my head was: 'Maybe today I will be going home,' but sadly that hope was just that, a hope, as I would find out later the same day. Thoughts ran through my mind like: 'How did I get to this point?' 'What had I done to deserve this?' 'I'm not crazy or insane, so why am I here why are they punishing me for nothing?' The tablet they gave me had worn off and I knew any chance of going back to that blissful sleep was over. Dreams of those fantasy places where the monsters of dreams reside. Those monsters escape me for yet another day till I return to that dreamland again at the end of the day. As I think of those monsters, my axe and my knives, a pleasure fills me. In those hours of my dreams I can be the monster and the monsters the victims. Knives flash, axes fly and in those dreaming hours, all monsters meet their demise. Their blood flows like water in that paradise land. Flesh cut from bone isn't it grand. Then as I awake, those glorious landscapes fade and those monsters of dreams get their reprieve for another day. In my dreams, my true nature is free and I can be all I need to be. Is that the dream and the dream world reality? I wish oh do I wish for those fantasy worlds and long beaches of golden sands and crystal seas. A place I could reside, wouldn't it be grand.

I made a note to myself; never to explore those dreams with anyone while I am in that place – especially not the doctors. As I dream, I enjoy and cherish what others might misinterpret or not understand. Those dreams of mine, I wonder if they might make good stories. In time I will document them all for you all to enjoy. Books of demons and monsters will follow and flow so you too can enjoy the dreams I have. I know from past experience, from discussing my dreams with family and friends, that my dreams disturbed them. If it had that effect on family and friends, what effect would it have on my doctor?

All there was to do was lie there, listening to the patients as some wake and others snore. Other patients that have problems howl, scream or cry; tormented souls fighting their own demons, and the sounds of the nurses talking and trying to ease the torment of these who are most afflicted.

A face appeared at the end of the bed; a nursing assistant. Don't you hate those people who are full of the joys of spring in the mornings? In my mind I hear her call, suggesting that I am the amusement and that I should say something to wipe that silly smile off her face. But then is she just echoing my own feelings and thoughts? No, I will play nice and not rock the boat. Making a mental note that before I leave that place, I will find a way to be the engineer of their demise and wipe that false smile of their faces. I incoherently mumbled the comments she was looking for, while thinking: 'I so want to give you a bad day.'

Slowly dragging my sore body out of the bed devised by torturers, the hard mattress had left my body stiff in places I hadn't known existed. I wondered if the beds had been designed to force the patients to get better so they could escape sleeping on them. Maybe they were just a way of getting a sick pleasure at the discomfort of the patients. As I climbed out of that bed, my desire to find the person who designed it and make them suffer the way we had, to let them sleep in their own diabolical torture device flared. I was definitely not in a nice mood.

Seven in the morning; it was time for a wash and to get ready for the day. My razor and shaving foam had vanished since I arrived. When I asked that sickening-pleasant nursing assistant, I found that they confiscated everything that could be seen as harmful. Checking through my bits, my mirror had gone as well as the little bag of 'therapeutic powder' I had buried in the bottom of the soap dish under my soap. It wasn't like I was going to take it, I wasn't addicted anymore but on the longest of days, I found amphetamines helped the day fly fast and subdue the worst of my demons. They had no right! It was not theirs to take away. I had only enough to escape for a day but they had taken it away. I was completely at the mercy of my demons with no form of escape. They had robbed me of the only chance of sanity and escape that I had. I knew I suffered to the point of addiction but I could handle it, I knew I could.

To shave, I had to queue up by a window and wait to be issued a safety razor that couldn't shave a peach. What was I, a naughty child who couldn't be trusted with a blade? As I entered the shower and bathroom, my mood took a further dive. The toilet stall had doors but under and above them light showed, anyone could look under or over - no privacy could be gleaned there. The sinks were in a row, the showers were communal and big baths were in centre of the room. You couldn't even lie in the bath in privacy. Were they serious or was it some type of sick joke? I had a wash, brushed my hair and teeth, made myself presentable for the day so I could wait for when they said I could go home. I went back to my bed and straightened it then went through the few clothes I had brought with me and selected something comfy to wear. Since John's demise, and meeting Catherine, I had taken to wearing black; it felt comfy and felt right, it fitted me like a glove. Light colours just didn't feel right. As my fingertips brushed against my hidden scars, my mind drifted back to Catherine and our times together. Those dark pleasures seemed like an eternity ago, how can fate be so cruel and unfair? As I sat there thinking of my sweet Catherine, a nursing assistant appeared and informed me that breakfast had arrived. I walked out to the main ward communal area and metal trolleys loaded with breakfast had appeared. Cereal, fry-ups, everything was there; scrambled eggs, bacon, fried bread, beans - anything you could want. Selecting a few morsels, I filled my plate then went to sit alone at one of the top tables. Two patients sat down next to me and started to chat. I replied in a half-hearted manner. They asked why I was there and I tried to tell them that I shouldn't be there, that I am not sick and nothing was the matter. To my surprise they gave me an understanding look and I realized we were brothers and sisters together, trapped in that prison of society's making. My plate was empty and I sat sipping my coffee, working out my plan of action to escape that torment.

Breakfast finished, I went to sit in a chair. There was a bookshelf full of old titles. I sat reading, not digesting a word but indulging in the pretence of reading. I was analyzing the world around me and those that resided in that world.

Everyone, apart from one or two of those who sat in the room appeared normal and were busy in conversation. Some were smoking or reading, doing jigsaw puzzles or just playing board games. One was sat at the windows, staring out. I could only surmise he was dreaming of some way out.

Sometime later, a doctor appeared and called me into a room. The first question was simple: why was I there? My reply was simple too: I shouldn't be there, nothing was wrong. He ran through the usual routine of questions: Do you feel like hurting yourself? How are you sleeping? How is your mood?

I simply nodded and said 'I am fine'.

"You tried to take your own life," the doctor replied. That sent alarm bells ringing in my ears. In my head, I thought of a thousand and one excuses. But instead I came up with a simple answer.

"I was drunk and it was a simple mistake to kill a head ache."

The doctor seemed to brush it off with a fleeting glance, like he had heard that one a thousand times before.

"While in hospital, you stared into open space and responded with 'we' instead of 'I' and showed many other signs that something is wrong," he said.

That comment sank in and I realized that I wouldn't be going home that day.

"You have been sectioned under Mental Health Act three and will be with us for a while as we try to help you overcome these problems." The doctor was so pleasant, I just wanted to scream.

"You can't keep me here. I've done nothing wrong. I haven't hurt anybody. It's my life and body to do as I will."

The doctor stood up and then replied, "I think we'll leave it there 'til you calm down and I'll write you up for something that hopefully will help you. We'll talk again in a day or two, after the medication has started to work." With that, he pressed a button on the desk and two ward orderlies came in and escorted me out.

As I walked out into the main ward, thousands of things flooded through my head. How can they treat me like a prisoner? I am not a criminal to be locked up. I ran to a window and looked out, thinking maybe it was a way to escape. Looking out, I realized I was two floors up and even if I tried, I doubt the windows would open wide enough.

Prisoners get a release date but in that place there was no release date. They keep you until they think you should be free, and even if you appeal, from what other patients told me, success was very unlikely.

I asked to get some fresh air in a faint hope and was told I could. Spirits raised and jacket on, and plans of escape in my mind. But as I got up, I was told there was a two on one escort for me at all times when I leave the ward. All plans I made of escape were sunk. It meant every time I went outside, a nurse and an orderly must accompany me. They didn't trust me not to do a runner or finish what I tried days before. That upset me an untold amount, but I could not let them see my dismay.

As we left the hospital building and entered the grounds, the fresh winter breeze rose up and caught my breath. Looking around the grounds, I saw it was a place of beauty and if it was not my prison, I might have enjoyed spending time there. Every step I took, I could feel their eyes watching for any sign that I might run. But that was far from what was running through my brain. If they wouldn't let me go I'd force them to or perish trying. Fighting and violence would not be the answer. Before I left the ward I saw an episode with a patient so I knew what the results would be. A patient had been upset and threw his weight around and before it could escalate, he was surrounded and sedated then moved to isolation. Knowing that fact, my choices were limited.

I knew what must be done; either they would let me out with a gentle protest or they would be carrying me out to a slab. Walking back in with my warders, I finalized the part of my plan that was to hopefully gain my freedom and escape from that place.

Getting back to the ward, sister was waiting; well she looked like a ward sister, I was never quite sure. She went through the basic rules: no drinking, no drugs unless proscribed and no fraternizing with female patients. Voluntary patients would be discharged if they broke the rules but section patients were put into segregation, or lockup as other patients liked to call it.

Most people were there for rest and minor things such as anxiety, sleep disorder or depression. Then there were a few with schizophrenia and other conditions, but no one was really a danger and if respected and treated right, was reasonably friendly. We did have one patient that might have been the exception; he was there because he loved fires. He wasn't scary and seemed a nice enough chap. I just made sure I didn't leave my lighter around him, better not risk tempting fate. Don't get me wrong, if he had burnt the place down and given me my escape, I would had the greatest of pleasure, I just didn't fancy it happening while I slept. It isn't as scary as it sounded, he was actually a very well-mannered, polite kid.

Late morning and another member of staff appeared on the ward; a pretty nursing assistant that I complimented. That was definitely a fatal mistake as I got a lecture for the next hour from a senior female member of staff about what is proper. I wondered if I could get her to take me out for a walk and if she would accidently fall down a flight of stairs. Then I realized it wasn't actually *my* thought; it was *her* deep in my head, putting ideas there. But I have admit, she didn't have a bad idea. I guessed an accident so soon after me arriving would be too obvious. Give it time, we can wait. There was always the chance of a perfect opportunity. Lecture over at long last, I returned to my reading.

While I was reading I saw staff rushing to the far end of the room. Screaming started and I saw it was a really nice girl called Amy making the noise. She was paranoid that bugs were watching her and another patient thought it would be amusing to drop a bug on her lap. It sent her fleeing. I watched as they held her so that a needle could be slid into her arm. She was gently lifted back to her room. Ward Sister made it known that the panic was over and the usual atmosphere returned. (Note to self; make sure I don't get caught if I flip out), I didn't fancy being sedated. I was told by the other patients that incidents like that were uncommon on our ward and were few and far between.

The days in that place passed slowly and I tried in every little way to fight my oppressors; even in the littlest things, such as leaving all my stuff over my bed or not putting things away. One day I woke with one of my headaches. Since the mugging, I had been getting them and still do to this day, they were not as you would think of a headache, but far worse. Imagine someone heating a poker and putting it inside your head - that is an understatement of the pain I feel, but nearest example I can give.

I had just started to climb out of my bed when an orderly put his hand on my shoulder. Not thinking and full of pain, I reacted. His wrist locked and over my shoulder he went. It was funny; he was like a piece of paper. I never knew I had that much strength in me. But even as he was hitting the ground, I heard alarms start to ring and doctors, nurses and orderlies swarmed in. I did try to say sorry and explain, but before I could, I felt myself man-handled and pinned down. Next, the bite and sting of a needle and the world turned hazy.

I don't know how long I was in that hazy world; I saw faces come and go but never really knew who or where I was. Each time it started to clear and I shouted out 'what are you doing to me?' another sting and the haze would return. It must have been some days that I went through that routine but after I stopped trying to shout and relaxed and let my head clear. I woke to find myself laid in a bed in a white room. No sheets belt or shoes; just walls and a bed, soft and white all around me.

Nurses came in from time to time to see I was ok and give me a pill that returned me back to my dream land. It continued for a few more days until finally the door opened and I was released back into the community. As they wheeled me back to the ward, all manner of thoughts went through my head. Like: Why did they put me through that? It was an accident; it wasn't like I meant to hurt him. Why wouldn't they let me explain?

They had succeeded in one thing; it strengthened my resolve not to let them break me, to force them to let me out. No way was I going to suffer more of the abuses of my freedom. I didn't ask or want to be there so why would they treat me that way? I would teach them one way or another. That was when my scheming really started.

# Chapter Six

# PLAN

The plan for my freedom took a few days to work out. It wasn't a complicated plan but I had to look at all the angles and check whether they could stop me. I had read about hunger strikes in prisons and other institutions and most got resolved. I had to look at who could stop me and how to remove those issues.

A week later, I got up, shaved, had a big breakfast and sat at my window, waiting. They might hold my body prisoner, but that didn't mean I was going to make it easy for them.

Late morning, I took a walk to enjoy the grounds. I spent some time with my warders as I sat at the cricket pavilion making sure in myself that I was ready for that step. Once started, I knew if I backed out, anything I threatened would never be taken seriously again.

Lunchtime arrived and it was time to put my plan into action. The metal dinner carts pulled in and the staff walked around, telling us it was time for our medication and lunch. I had not been written up for meds then so I continued reading. Staff pointed out that dinner was there a few times and that I should eat, but I refused. Finally the sister came over for a chat.

"If you are refusing to eat, you might extend your stay here," she said.

I was half expecting that, so I shrugged my shoulders and went back to my book. A nursing assistant brought an observation machine and took my stats then led me to a scale to weigh me.

The next part of the plan was to remove all backup they had from the equation. My family was their only form of backup against my actions. After a phone call to my solicitor and a short chat, he explained that my family was trying to keep me there. Papers were then filed and actions taken to divorce my family and all rights to intercede were removed. It would be some days before the hospital found out. My plan had started and there was no way I would back out and show them I was weak. For the rest of the afternoon, I drank plenty of tea and coffee, making sure that it was loaded with sugar. Once or twice, staff came over to ask if I wanted to do some art, or play a game. I totally ignored them.

I spent the rest of the day lost in my books. The evening meal came and I refused to eat again. Staff started to see it as no more than an idle threat and decide to humour me. After dinner, the doctor appeared and I was once again led to his room. His comments are not even worth mentioning; he spent ages saying what could be relayed in a few words. I'll give you the condensed and less boring version instead. His was a lecture on how dangerous my course of action was and how it would affect my recovery. Big deal! If it wasn't dangerous, I wouldn't be trying it. What did they think I was, stupid? So what? Should I just give up after a few words from them? No way. It showed I was finally getting to them and that route might be the right one.

I didn't know at the time how right they were, or how I'd open Pandora's Box and cause a change that would last forever. The days that followed were the same; morning they would offer me breakfast, I'd decline it and then I would sit by the window with my book or watch outside till lunch then decline that too. My observations and weight would be checked and I would go back to my window and books again. At first I found release from it all by walking the grounds with a nurse. Finding a place to sit and watch the trees or the sky. We talked for hours about life, trees and everything apart from my actions.

After a few days, everything became more of a chore. The temperature of the ward was dropping, I wondered if they were trying to freeze me out of my plan. If I complained to the staff, they would say the ward temperature was ok and if I would eat I'd soon feel warmer. Did they really think I was so stupid that I'd fall for that one? Hot tea with sugar helped warm me up a bit but it wasn't a solution. My weight was dropping; 3 pounds in the first week and I looked good. Why hadn't I tried it long time ago?

At first, every time I saw food, I would have to force myself not to want it, but as time went on, food started to revolt me. The smell, the look; even the idea made my stomach turn. I no longer remembered how many days it had been since I last tasted food. Time moved on and the staff kept watching me, hoping I would break, but I refused to give them the satisfaction.

The other patients were no longer happy to see me; they had sorrow in their eyes. Why should they feel sorry for me? I was winning; soon the system would break and I would be free. Going outside was no longer an option; the cold air froze me to the bone and even the softest surface felt hard and cold. I did miss walking those grounds but I just couldn't manage it, even the stairs were too much of a chore. The last time I tried, I got four stairs down and almost had to be carried back to the ward.

It had been a few weeks and I noticed a smell of acetone. Was it on the ward or my clothes? I realised it was coming from me. My trips to the lavatory had reduced too, I thought maybe my body might have been starting to slow. I thought I saw red in my urine, maybe it was just my eyes playing tricks. I had had a bit of a blur occasionally the previous day or so. My stools had become solid and I found them hard to pass - like solid brown pebbles when I passed them at all. My own bowels were starting to betray me.

The hospital got the papers to confirm my family was divorced from me and no longer had a say in my care. Doctors and nurses realised at last that I meant to carry out my plan and held a meeting on what action they could legally take. I was told the meeting was taking place but was not privy to attend. I knew they were planning something, but no one would let slip what it was.

I started the action to be free - one way or the other - and was slowly realizing that it might be the other. I had gone too far to turn back even if I wanted to, even if I did feel weak. Even the idea of eating made me feel sick. I lost track how many days it had been and how many lectures I had been given. The staff stopped lecturing me but rather seemed like vultures in wait.

I had stopped brushing my hair. It had turned brittle and with every brush stroke I seemed to have less. My nails changed too; lighter, more fragile and brittle. I no longer read my books as a lot of the time I found my mind wandering back to earlier years and the time my brother and I had spent together. It was becoming a chore to make my diary entries. My sleep was no longer sound; rather it was disturbed by constant chattering in the recesses of my mind.

Sister told me my mother phoned and asked how I was. They did as I first instructed and told her I was as well as could be expected and that legally they could give her no further answers. My family had no idea what was going on in the four walls of the hospital and the staff couldn't inform them as I was over eighteen; and so they remained in oblivious bliss. All they knew was that I cut them off as they were unwanted. In my opinion, it was for the best. I knew they were not going to like it one bit.

Mornings were getting harder; I was so tired all the time that it was an effort to get out of bed; my legs started to fail me. One morning I tried to get up and stand and they gave out on me and I laid there until staff nurse came and got me. Even my own body was turning against me, betraying me at every turn. I found that I slept longer and took more naps in the day. I didn't know how much longer my fingers would allow me to make further entries. My weight loss was prominent; my skin was loose and my eyes had receded. Where there once was fat on my cheek, looked like just bone. My ribs had become visible too. I looked like one of those pictures of the third world.

The nurse wheeled me in a chair to my windows and I watched outside and drank my sweet tea through a straw. My skin had started to crack and was brittle as I tried to rub cream into it, though my fingers felt so heavy and weak. I heard sister tell one ward assistant 'not long now'. Was I winning? Were they going to give in? But deep inside, I knew I had gone way too far and that even if they did give in, I couldn't reverse it, and had to let the course of my action play out.

Three more days went past and I could no longer leave my bed. I just couldn't stand on my legs or sit in a chair anymore; they betrayed me at every turn. Why did I bother keeping them when they were no longer any good to me? The previous night as I was half asleep, my brother came to see me. He'd been dead for some time of course, but he was there, I know he was. He sat on my bed and we talked about happier times and I told him how much I missed him; before I went to sleep, I missed him so.

My observations were no longer done daily but hourly and each time they were done, the nurse just nodded to sister. I was told that I was shutting down and that I needed to take something, even if it was a sip of food supplement. I tried to shout out 'NO' but it came out in no more than a whisper.

I lay there, not moving, just watching everyone - patients and staff. Patients just bowed their heads as they walked past my bed. Later in the day they rolled my bed to a solitary room so I could be alone and no patient could disturb me.

I missed seeing the other patients' faces and hearing their voices. The blankets were no longer warming me so nurse covered me with more. It helped a little but they felt so heavy and there was still a chill in my bones.

I would have liked to go more in-depth on this matter, but pages are short and the story is long so I am sorry it is just the highlights.

As I lay there, I wondered where I would go. I have sinned so much and I was brought up catholic. I know my sins don't matter as the final act of starvation means I will be denied a catholic funeral and my soul will be barred from heaven. But then would I want go there knowing there would be no drinking, gambling or lust, for eternity? That would be torture. I smiled to myself as I thought that. My eyes were getting heavy, I felt so tired. I thought that might be my last entry.

If I don't wake and you are the person who reads this, please keep it safe and remember me. The pen tends to slip from my fingers. It was once so light, now it's like a weight. I am panting to breathe and my chest feels so heavy and weak.

At 9:15 that night, I passed into a deep sleep, one my body was too weak to wake from. I heard after that they had taken me to a local hospital where I could receive vital medical care. They put me on drips and fed me through tubes through my nose. My metabolism had slowed down to much they were scared of me totally shutting down. For days, if not weeks I laid in that state. Machines and warming blankets kept me going at first, till my body was strong enough to take over. Yet on I slept. It turned out that they had that eventuality planned for days before my passing out and had the hospital on standby to receive me.

# Chapter Seven

# DEMON WORLD

I remember some of the dream I had, but some of that time after I first awoke is lost to me. The relevance of this dream will be seen by the end of the story.

After I went into my deep sleep, I was trapped between two places; one of light and as I stared into that place, there were shadowy beings and shapes moving. Behind me was a dark place that seemed to swallow the light. Looking at the light it seemed to call out to me but it was too bright, I couldn't go that way. The light blinded my soul like it was repulsing me. I turned instead to the welcoming darkness. As I moved forward, the darkness embraced me. I felt safe, covered and hidden from the light trying to find me.

I walked further into the darkness, the light behind me faded until it was totally gone. The end of the tunnel was finally in sight. What was under my feet was solid yet not solid. It was as though I was walking on dark clouds of smoke - spongy under my feet.

Onwards I walked and a pale purple colour appeared at the end of the tunnel in the distance. It was a blur at first but as I moved forwards it grew brighter and brighter 'til it filled the end of the tunnel and my vision. Speeding up, I moved faster towards the pale purple light. Have you ever had the feeling that where you were going was right? The moment I saw that purple sky ahead of me I knew I was going in the right direction.

Time was not measurable but if I had to put a time on it, the final part of the walk must have taken an hour. As I approached the end of the tunnel, I could make out a black terrain and a sky that was purple and pale; so much beauty I had never known. My last step away from that tunnel led my feet to walk upon stone. Looking back, the tunnel had gone and where I stood was a platform of mirrored black stone. Where the tunnel had been there was an obelisk of stone with golden writing standing eight foot tall.

Looking up, I saw something I could only have dreamed; the sun and the moon side by side in the sky. A sun radiating purple light and the moon glistening like a black diamond.

I do understand that it was just a dream, but it was a dream that felt so real. On the floor, beyond the end of the stone plinth was a landscape with stark and strange lava formations through fields of black sand bare of vegetation. With the sun's purple light blazing, I decided to wait beneath the shade of some type of tree just ahead.

Reaching down, I scooped up a handful of sand and as it ran through my fingers, it sparkled. Not like the sand I had always known, but rather a sand of pulverised black diamonds. Then I saw it; stretched across the southern sky, more than halfway to the horizon, was a heavenly sight, a belt or some type of halo. A combination of colours that defied belief, red, gold, blue and deep purples - too many colours to name; a flowing softness moving but stationary, it gave the feeling it was alive. The sight before me had me perplexed and mystified. I had never seen a sight like it! It was vibrant.

Hypnotic in nature, calling me near, my feet started moving forward. I walked; all power of will had been taken away. Not a thought entered my head except to follow and get there. What was that beauty ahead that held me so tight? Forward I walked; not a care in the world, the only thought in my head was my final destination. Then as I was walking forward I must have missed my footing because I slid forward down a bank. I was skidding onto my face. In an instant I was free in the hold of that light. Sorrow filled my very being; temptation to look back at it was filling my mind, 'no I must not give in, I must stay strong and avoid looking or risk being lost in its beauty forever', I thought.

As I sat there trying to regain my bearings and thinking about that, I was reminded of my hunting trips as a child and how I would snare an animal by offering it what it desired. Was it a light ahead of me or a snare of a type that no mortal man could escape? If so, how many had come before me and succumbed as I nearly did? But then did it matter as it was only a dream and wasn't real, but something inside was uneasy and warned me that I had to be better safe than sorry. If I was trapped there would I ever awake?

I sat for some time, watching the sky and waiting for the air to cool. I was careful not to glance at the halo in the distance. Rope and wire snares set by humans were used to catch animals in order to feed. Was that a type of snare designed or created to catch and feed on humans and other beings like me? Part of me wanted to flee to the safety of the dark, blank sandy seas, but I knew if I ever was to awake, my only choice was to explore the origin of the snare and find some way to escape.

Moving forward, careful to shield my eyes from the mesmerizing light, I carried on my journey heading slowly towards it. Hours passed as I walked and day turned into total night; the sun was no longer visible but for a purple glow round the moon like the eclipses on earth. Unable to see more than a few feet in front of me, I settled in a hole between some rocks. In the darkness a chattering could be heard. I cried out, 'Who's there?' but received no response. Reaching around me, I found and gathered some scrub and wood. Not knowing if flint existed there, I picked up different stones and struck them together. Again and again I tried to make a spark but to no avail until I found some silvery grey stones. At the first stroke I felt them warm, and with a second, they burst into flame. Instantly I dropped them, escaping with no more than a singe. The stones burned with a pale flame but I had no more fuel and before I could act, the fire died. Maybe they were similar to magnesium that I once played with as a boy at school?

Searching around, I found two more of the grey stones and I placed one in the centre of the scrub and smashed the other into it over and over 'til it ignited then I dropped it. As it burned and ignited the scrub, I remember thinking, 'If this is a dream and my body is not here, would I burn?' Common sense took over and I was unwilling to put it to the test. Instead, with my fire alight and keeping those distant chattering voices at bay, I added more scrub and settled for the long night. If it wasn't a dream, I'd have said I slept a sound sleep 'til daybreak but all I know is it can't have been anything but a dream.

When I awoke, I felt stiff from sleeping on the sand. The fire was no more, just warm embers remained. I set off on my journey. As I walked, I saw trails in the ground like little footprints. Could they have been made by my visitors in the night? Finding a few more silver stones, I put them in my nightshirt pocket. Onwards I walked 'til I came to a black pond that looked like water. I cupped my hands and lifted some out. It felt heavy and looked less transparent than water but a sip told me that indeed it was drinkable.

I had fire and drinking water; two things to survive and all I needed then was food and I'd be alright. On a bush I found what looked like some kind of fruit. It was black and yellowish and such a sickly colour. Hunger clawed at my stomach and I gently bit into one. With flesh as hard as leather and hairs on its skin as prickly as needles, I could not bite through. Scarce as the bushes were, it seemed that was all that grew.

In final desperation, I picked up two large rocks and smashed the fruit between them. As the fruit split, I was rewarded with a smell as sweet as honey and bright red flesh flowed out. Dipping one finger in and tasting it, I expected the fruit to taste like its shell but instead was rewarded with a taste that rivalled the nectar of the gods. Having once eaten the food of the underworld, could I ever be free of the place with that addictive nectar always drawing me back to taste of that fruit once more?

That world was plunged into a darkness that swallows the light at night and into a barren wasteland barely containing life during the day, but when I returned to my body, no produce; flowers, fruit, or grain could ever compare to the smell and taste of the fruit I tasted that day.

Refreshed and renewed with energy I had never felt before, I walked on though the wilderness; through fields of dark grasses and scrubs. Occasionally I caught site of a stream flowing dark and slow. The only animals I saw were not animals as anyone could call them. Rather, they were lumbering demonic beasts with talons for fingers and hides of bruised-looking leather. Black, cracked, filthy bones protruded from their seeping skin. Their arms were thin and spindly, oozing purple, rotten slime. Others were eight foot tall, eye sockets as dark as Hades and skin that looked alive, crawling over their vast shell-like bodies. Their misshapen reptile-like heads held numerous rows of diamond teeth.

Then you had others, the shapeless ones that at a distance looked like a cloud of black sands. As they approached the others, they formed into indescribable shapes with glowing red eyes, devouring their victims before turning back to clouds of black dust, leaving nothing but picked-clean bones. I called those creatures the formless ones or shape-shifters; not being able to decide on which name suited them best. I had to watch every step to make sure that none crossed my path.

Then there were human-shaped ones that wandered the wastelands. Not going in any particular direction, just walking and screaming like men in mortal torment. Looking at them, if I didn't know better, I could have mistaken them for humans grossly mutilated; they seemed to be preyed on by all.

Walking on, trying to avoid the beasts, I constantly looked around. For some time I saw nothing, the feeling of security once again returned. However moments later, as if they had materialized from nothing, I saw them just ahead. I watched, waited and listened for a while to see if they detected me. A group of human-shaped beasts headed towards me. A beast disappeared and rematerialized behind the human-shaped things and as it was about to kill them, a dark cloud flowed up, seemingly from out of the ground and surprised them. It gave enough time for the creature to tear through the humans, before disappearing into the cloud accompanied by unholy screams that filled the air. Shaken to the core, I staggered on, never in my life imagining such brutality could exist.

There was a strange grace and beauty in their movements. Even in the act of such violence, there was grace; each cut, every slice was like a graceful dance of death. Beasts such as them should have been slow and cumbersome but instead they moved so fast and light; almost like every movement flowed. I warned myself not to underestimate them. If they could be that graceful in the kill, how fast and graceful would they be on the run if ever it came to chasing me down?

Once I had seen beauty in the demon world I travelled, but after those experiences, it could only be described as a nexus of hell. Could I escape or would it be my home for eternity? Water was abundant, food was fantastic, and I had fire and warmth so I had the necessary tools to survive.

Suddenly dark shadows surrounded me, striking out from their dark place, cutting my skin making me bleed. I screamed as a dark fire burned through my very skin. A cold white hand grabbed my wrist pulling me free. A scream went up from the shape-shifter and it became solid rather than the dark cloud it had been. Its eyes were like fire, standing six foot tall, skin plated with black diamond.

My saviour roared back and then I realized he wasn't my saviour; he didn't want to miss out on a meal. Gathering my wits, I ran for an outcrop ahead. Behind me, the air was full of screams of rage and the battle between the two beasts. As I ran, I dared not look back in case the battle was won and I was to be the next course.

Screams filled the air as I neared the base of the tunnel. Piercing cries came up the dark tunnel to meet me. I could feel fear, death and sin all around me. As I moved down the tunnel all those soulless voices appeared ahead of me as corpses, pieces of rotting meat that were hung from hooks on either side of the tunnel's walls. Could there be a more cruel fate than for a soul to regain a body only to feel it rot away day by day, helpless and hopeless? Cries of those dammed souls reached into my own soul.

Inching forward step by step, fighting the terror and despair, the cries of the damned drove me near to panic. Walking into the main chamber of what can only be called a maze, the voices started to fade. When entering, I noticed that there were many paths leading off in all directions from the entrance. From two of the tunnels, I heard the sounds that had filled me with dread on the dark nights I had previously survived. The chattering sound that placed images in my mind of swarms of creatures ready to rush me and tear me to ribbons. The first two paths were blocked by rivers of lava. The third path was clear. As I walked the path, it was leading away from the other paths. The farther I walked, the more the walls seemed to heat and a sulphur smell filled the air. Sweating and exhausted, I moved forward till the path ahead opened out into a great cavern where hot lava flowed deep below. I was standing on a great bridge spanning across between giant cavern walls that towered over me on all sides. Hidden by shadow at the far end was an entrance that would lead to me to escape. Out of the darkness, shadows moved and faded, to be replaced by a face, a face of darkness with red, fiery eyes that burned into my very soul until they became a living nightmare that could drag you to hell and haunt your dreams forever. Slowly, what once was shadow, somehow formed and solidified to become the shape of a man, with garments as black as night. A shape-shifter had found me and thought that the best way to catch me was to take my own form.

The heat and lava made moving forward a perilous task. Not far behind, the dark spectre of a man followed fast and strong. Tunnel after tunnel, his steps could be heard behind, never moving further forward or back.

Then I caught the worst odour that could have ever been

smelled. It was the smell of decaying souls, and it seemed to be coming from every direction. Moving forward, I entered an open space with purple daylight streaming in from far ahead. The spectre behind howled in fury then fled. What could scare a creature as evil as that and make him flee?

Walking into the pale purple light, I came out on an outcrop. Before me was a wide circular valley. Lava filled the floor way below me. The walls were reflecting a multi-coloured spectrum. I was scared to look up in case it was what I feared. The halo! It must be far above me.

Seven pillars were standing tall like great beasts in the sea of lava. On the head of each of those beasts were ten gold rings that looked like majestic crowns. Each crown had a chain linking to a platform in the centre of the roof high above me. Far below were humanoid shapes; their flesh and blood had been left in their earthly graves. All that remained was the shape of their former beings, yet the stench of decay filled the air. No flesh remained to rot or decompose. The stench was that of those twisted souls and the rottenness of the sins they had carried out in their lives. Demonic worms crawled over the souls, feeding on all the goodness that remained. Souls were fighting and screaming to get away from the feast that they had become.

I watched, helpless and filled with a sense of frustration as a thousand tormented souls, man woman and child were devoured by those worms.

Never in my life have I sensed such evil or despair as I did standing there. Wickedness seemed to permeate the very air. Their cries of anguish vibrated in the rock like an orchestra of the damned, filling the air like a deafening sea of sound.

I was right, the halo was a trap, a trap to bring the sinners' souls to that desecrated ground.

Many others were being tortured by demons. Those who

escaped the worms headed to the centre of the lake where searing fires burned, only to be tortured by other demons. What was left of the bodies was stripped away and only the dark red light of their souls remained.

Watching those flames and the demons using their razor claws to rip the bodies away from the souls, even though the bodies weren't those of flesh and blood, just a morphic field or projection, I could still smell their rotting, putrid stench and hear the deafening screams.

Demons of all sizes were having a feeding frenzy, feasting on a never-ending pool of humanity. Every so often, as I watched, they came across a soul they couldn't strip; they were carried to a platform way above. That was followed by a scream that defied belief, but unlike the souls that sank as pale red lights into the sea of lava once devoured, to burn in extreme torment for eternity, those souls never came down. Instead, they were devoured by a creature far above.

Looking around, I noticed some holes in the rock face to which I climbed up. Hand over foot, I clambered higher and higher. Looking down to see if the dark figure was following, I saw the unquenchable fire far below and the sea of souls in agony. All manner of tortures inflicted upon them by the terrorizing demons.

As I climbed higher, the heat from below turned the cooler air to cloud. Lightning flickered from each of the great beasts' majestic crowns to something way above. It was then that it finally dawned on me that I could have been in hell.

The halo wasn't there just to trap sinful souls but a prison that also held the warders. Walled on all sides, and lightning above, nothing larger than a man could escape. The halo wasn't just a magnet to the sinners who entered that world, it was also a wall to keep the warders in. Unlike man, those brutes had no eyelids to close and escape its hypnotic pull.

Climbing yet higher, I finally saw the real prisoner of the hell jail. Sitting on a throne as dark as night, in the centre of the platform sat a figure; a large creature, at least eighteen feet in height with black shining wings eight foot long. It had a dark body that could only be described as perfect in its beauty. Shaped like a man, but not a man as you would expect, he was perfect in all proportions. Its body was adorned with precious jewels and his eyes glistened like stars.

The platform was made of what first looked like silver tiles. But as I looked, I saw one tile rise and a demon brought a soul from below. Chains flew out, enveloped the soul and pulled it in and then the tile sunk back into the platform. Climbing faster, I tried to escape before I was seen but I was too late. As I got to the top of the wall, a great hand reached up and grabbed me, pulling me back down.

Looking into that perfect face, all fear left me and a sense of peace filled me. Chains flew out around me, hooks bit into my flesh as I was pulled back. Inch by inch the chains pulled me in. It was too late for escape and I fought the chains 'til I too was sealed in my cold metal coffin. I screamed but no one listened as the doors shut and I felt it lower down into my eternal tomb. Darkness engulfed me and my mind began to swim.

Then voices came from a long distance away, pulling my mind towards them. Brightness surrounded me then the voices became clearer.

# Chapter Eight

# AWAKENING

I heard voices as I awoke but I couldn't understand what was being said. I could just make out blurred images of different faces looking down at me then moving away before darkness engulfed me again. My consciousness came and went and I couldn't tell if I was still dreaming or not. Was I still trapped in that metal box, was it all an illusion?

The next feeling I had was that of my body being moved around and the blurred images and voices were back. I lay there forever, sometimes groaning when I exhaled, just to hear something.

Gradually everything became a little clearer. I started to be aware of more every time I woke but then I drifted back into darkness. I realized I was in a hospital bed and something was tugging on my nose. As I tried to raise my hands to pull the thing from my nose that was bugging me, I realized that my hands were strapped down and there were two rails on either side of the bed stopping me from rolling off. I tried to make sense of things then I remembered my long dreams and a shudder went through my bones. Not a dream or a place I would like to go to again. Was it a dream? It seemed so real. Wanting my hands to be free, I saw someone in uniform come in and I thought it was a nurse. I tried to talk to her. She looked at me then pressed a button. Next minute I was surrounded by doctors and nurses. Lights were shone in my eyes and pins prodded into my fingers and toes.

"Can you feel this?" a doctor asked as he prodded in different places. I wanted to cry out, 'Of course I can, stupid!' but instead, a weak and feeble, "Yes" left my lips and I lay there too exhausted to moan or complain.

"Do you know your name?" The doctor asked me. As I tried to answer, my voice was still no more than a whisper. Still confused, I wondered what was going on.

My first name was easy but my second took some work as my brain was trying to process all the new information. After a few moments, I managed to recall my last name and with that I was left alone to comprehend the situation and what was going on.

Where was I? How did I get there? Then faint memories of the asylum and starving myself filtered through my addled mind. My last memory was fading into darkness in my bed in the asylum then the weird dream. Wasn't I in the asylum? Why was I tied down? I had never tried to hurt myself or anyone other than the starvation. I knew I was in a hospital but what type of hospital was it?

Nurses came in and cleaned me up. I had been asleep so long they had to use pads under me. The drips in my arms were being disconnected. My memory was sketchy but in time it returned. The therapist came in to help me get out of bed. From the starvation then the long sleep, my legs and arms were extremely weak. I began to insist that I be allowed to walk so I could use the bathroom. At one point, the nursing staff had to hoist me onto a chair and wheel me into the toilet. You wouldn't believe how much humility you learn when you are that reliant on others. That was when I realized the damage I had done to myself and how weak I had become through my own stubbornness and stupidity.

I had tried to force them to give into me, yet all I succeeded in doing was to make myself weak. I had gone from being strong and in control to being as weak as a toddler. My action didn't force them to let me go; instead it put me at their mercy. I couldn't even get to the bathroom without their aid. I felt humiliated if not ashamed. I know I don't have full range of emotions but those are some I am pretty sure I did find. I was like a child learning to walk, but as time went on, my legs got stronger and I was walking unaided. Food was a problem as I couldn't keep down solids. My body and mind became accustomed to me not eating and while asleep, the nasogastric tubes had fed me. Even the tiniest morsel made me want to retch. Every day I ended up saying, 'I can't do this.' But as the days went by, I was allowed to eat real food but seemed to be full after only a few bites. My sense of taste and smell no longer seem to work very well. I went from the tiniest crumb to eating a small meal again and then back to normal. That didn't happen over days, it took weeks. Then came the day the Neurological Rehab ward said I was ready to go. I wasn't sure who was most relieved, me or the asylum. While I was in hospital, one of their staff had to stay with me to make sure I was ok but staff was removed when I was released.

My dream while I was asleep haunted me, it had seemed too real and I wasn't in a hurry to return to that place. Any thoughts or Ideas of starving myself again was out of my head. I decided living was a better option than the alternative. I know it seems silly for a dream to change things but you would have had to have lived that dream to know why it had such an effect on me. My trip back to the asylum seemed longer than the first time. I was actually looking forward to it and seeing the patients that I grew to care about during my time there. As I was wheeled into the ward, faces turned to me. The staff welcomed me back and the patients hugged me.

I was settled in that day and when dinner call sounded, I made sure I was first in the queue; much to the amusement of the other patients.

'You going to leave some for us?' was the jokey comment I got from a few as I filled my plate to over-flowing. That plate of food tasted like a gift from the gods. After dinner, I sat by the main table, chatting to patients, finding out who had left and who was new. I don't know if it was the meds that they had put me on while I was asleep that had started to work or not, but that place no longer felt like a prison.

When I first got here I had an aversion to being caged and tied to and locked in that place. I would look out of the window with longing and watch visitors and staff go home. I would long to be one of them to be set free. That was my goal but the plan had backfired so drastically. I longed just to feel the sun on my skin and the wind in my face, but due to my action, it would be some time before I would be able to.

There was no way I was going to give the staff an easy time; no way would I let them know they had me. Plans were formed within plans to teach them that they couldn't hold me. Nervously I went to sleep praying I wouldn't go back to that place. The nurse who checked on me saw how nervous I was about sleeping.

"Dreams can't hurt you," she said.

"You want to bet? Dream what I had and you'd be in no doubt!" I replied.

She then offered me something to help me to sleep. I took it gratefully. Soon I slipped into a dreamless slumber.

I woke at seven the next morning, still feeling a bit drowsy from the pill they gave me. It felt good to be back in my bed. OK, maybe not *my* bed but a bed that wasn't at that hospital with all the tubes and pipes. After a supervised wash and shave, I went for breakfast. A breakfast of kings! Bacon, eggs, hash browns, tomatoes, beans, fried bread, and black pudding. I wasn't going to miss out on anything put in front of me. It was a shame, for some reason my taste buds didn't quiet seem back to normal; nothing tasted exactly like I remembered.

After breakfast, I went and played a few hands of cards with Jesus and Kim. Jesus was so down to earth and funny. His real name wasn't Jesus, it was James but he believed he was the son of God and named Jesus. It was hard to understand why he had been sectioned and put there. He was kind, polite and had nothing but good things to say, apart from believing he was Jesus he had nothing wrong with him. Kim was as down to earth as you could get but suffered from clinical depression. Some days she could be ok and a real joy to be with but other days, darkness descended and not a word would she utter. On those bad days, we would drag her into a game and try to see if we could put that smile on her face again.

It's amazing how throwing a few hands of cards away would help someone's mood, but then Kim was the link-pin that held in place the fragile equilibrium that had become my life. If I was having a black day and the clouds were surrounding me, she would run defence for me, keeping other patients and doctors at bay. I have to admit, thinking back, she was a special woman. After she left that place, we lost contact over time. Her family moved her to a rehabilitation centre or as I would call, it a 'small community' somewhere and they felt contact with her past was not a good thing. So letters stopped arriving and gradually she became part of my past. But so long as I'm alive I will always be grateful to the part she had played in everything during my darkest times.

In the days that followed, my body slowly finished its repairs. Occasionally I would feel an odd twinge of cold. That dream I had when I was starving still bothered me a bit, but my fear of it faded as it didn't reappear. I found out that while I was passed out, I went into cardiac failure and they had to fight to bring me back. Years later, I still have bald patches on my chest where the hair has never grown back in those two places. That shouldn't have happened.

Was it a dream, was it a hallucination or was it part of the period I was dead? I won't know the answer to that question until my time comes to an end. When it does come, I have to admit, I do hope I find out it was a dream or hallucination. The thought of an eternity in that place would be too much to bear.

Since that dream, I developed a new philosophy on life; mutual karma - neither good nor bad, I try to keep on the knife's edge as they say; an equal balance between all the good and harm I might do.

# Chapter Nine

# SURRENDER

It was during that time, while I was in the hospital that I actually had some of the best times of my life; I started to fit in like a glove. Around me were others of my kind; they were diagnosed and they recognized, despite my efforts to hide it, they saw my Dark side. The chlorpromazine and the molipaxin they gave me partially silenced the voices of darkness in my mind and helped me gain control of myself again. The other patients started to seem more normal to me and saner than those in the outside world.

During that time, I met a girl who was the same as me; someone who could understand what was inside me. Once I was allowed to walk the grounds, the two of us went everywhere and talked about everything in our lives. She was similar to me; a death and trying to take her life had brought the voice to her like a demon from the void. She too had fought the voices for a long time, only to finally lose to them. Not being able to cope anymore, she took her father's razor and ran a bath. She soaked in the water and slid the razor across both wrists. It's only the fact that the blade was fairly blunt and her mother and father heard the blade drop that she survived. She too had fought the system and the doctors when she had got there and had finally come round once the meds had sunk in.

We spent many a day walking the grounds, just chatting about anything and everything. If you had looked at us, you wouldn't be able to see that we were any different than normal people. The paranoid feeling that we were being watched never left us but then maybe in that place we *were* being watched.

One cold winter's afternoon, behind the cricket pavilion, we shared our first kiss. I had kissed many girls in my youth but that was a kiss of urgency and need. After all the time when we had felt little or nothing, we both craved to feel something and that drove us on. Slowly we undressed each other then made mad, passionate love. Love might be the wrong word as to us 'love' is a thing we find hard to understand. Sarah was gentle yet passionate, her need for it radiated through all our actions.

With Catherine in Paris, it had been dark, unforbidden pleasures but with Sarah, it was gentle need and urgency. We made love 'til we were completely and physically drained. Then we held each other close. The world sees us as damaged minds that need to be fixed, but in those moments of being cuddled up together, the world seemed right. I lay there wondering what it would feel like if we were both normal and we made love but then I thought, 'who wants to be normal?' What we shared was special to us. Happy is one emotion we can feel and that filled us with a happiness we so rarely felt. The one concern I did have was the fact we had no birth control, but she shrugged it off. Did we do right, risking bringing another like us into the damaged world where our kind was locked up, stigmatized and seen as sick, damaged or crazy? To us it was those labelled as 'normal' that were the ones that were wrong. If anything, we don't do greed, jealousy or anger, so I ask you who are the real sick ones, us who have none of those depraved emotions or the ones who call themselves normal and suffer all those traits?

If the staff knew half of what we got up to that day they would have blown a fuse. Sadly our closeness was short-lived as Sarah was moved to a secure lockup unit. They said she was a danger and needed a secure unit. She wasn't a danger to us, she was so kind and gentle, it wasn't her fault the 'norms' caused her to lose herself and her inner self came out.

I think the fact that we both had similar problems helped us and that's what made us close. It was just that the drugs didn't control her inner demons and even though she was ok with us patients, the members of staff were always fearful around her; what if she decided to turn?

I still remember our last minutes together. I gave her a hug and a kiss and said goodbye as they took her to the transport. I did try and contact her, but only got one reply telling me to remember what we had and forget her. After that, all my letters were returned.

After she left, the hospital became an empty and desolate place. My main reason for tolerating it was gone and even though I cared as much as I could care for the other patients I called friends, I knew it was time I moved on.

I decided to get free. I knew there were two ways to get out - well three if you included the tribunal, but that would have been a futile option. Apart from giving them a headache at the effort to set it up and the report writing they would have to do afterwards, I have heard of a few who tried it but not heard of one who succeeded. The second was escape; it would have been simple, there was only one door on the ward between me and freedom and it would be so easy to wait 'til it was opened and dart out to freedom.

All I had to do was look innocent, maybe find something near the door that looked legit; there were always doctors and nurses, patients and relatives coming in and out, it would be so easy to slip past. But that would have put an alert out and I wouldn't have got far.

Instead, I chose to ask for a day's leave to see my family. The hospital knew I had divorced my family before I tried to starve myself, so I made the big deal about it being time I apologized and fixed things. That worked wonders as the doctors patted themselves on the back thinking I had made a breakthrough; but inside, I was planning a break-out.

I was given a ticket to get me home and instructions to call if I had any problems. In London I had to change to the train that was meant to get me home, but I never got on that train. Instead, I boarded a train going north. It was a long journey and I had time to think about things. Twice in recent years I had found a woman who had become special and twice fate had taken her away. Was I destined never to be lucky in that way?

I arrived in South Shields late that evening. It was a place that I knew from my childhood as I had an aunt there and always heard good things. I knew I couldn't visit her in case I was found, but it was a place I could be free.

The snow was coming down and I was beginning to feel the cold, so I started to walk. It was too late to find anywhere to stay, so I decided just find somewhere covered to rest 'til the break of day.

I walked 'til I came upon an alleyway. Through the alleyway was a sight I'll never forget; rocks and a vast ocean. Marsden rock was a place of natural splendour and beauty. In later years it would become my place of escape when the inner demons or life got too much. But that moment, as the silence filled the air and I sat in an alcove in the rocks, I felt such peace. All around me was a white wilderness.

There was the rubbish that kids and humans had dropped, with a few bits of wood dragged in by the ocean. With my lighter, I set light to the paper and it went up, soon followed by the driftwood. Shadows danced around the walls of the alcove as it burned and the only sound was the crackling of the fire as the salt from the ocean it had absorbed burned. Looking at the sea below, I felt so small, so peaceful like a speck on the ocean of life.

All that had happened in my life was tiny compared to the massive expanse of water that filled my view. Snow came down heavier and I watched as each flake touched the ocean and melted. The ocean was humanity and I was that little flake, fighting, locked away in a hospital, just melting into the background of life. I didn't want to melt away to nothing. I wanted to be part of the ocean; I wanted to been seen and heard not just forgotten.

It was during that long night sat in my alcove, watching the ocean, that I finally made peace with what I was and accepted my inner demons. As daybreak loomed, I walked back to the train station and boarded a train to where I had come from. I felt different inside, like a weight had been lifted from me. She was still there, telling me not to go, not to do it, but I ignored her and went back all the same.

I arrived at the train station near the asylum at 8pm at night, snow was coming down. The ground was white as far as the eye could see. It felt perfect as I walked through the snow, back to the asylum and what was becoming my long journey home. As I walked up the long drive, part of me wanted to turn and run, but another side told me I would never be free unless I went back.

When I entered the ward, I saw faces light up and all around other patients welcomed me back warmly. Exhausted, I retired to my bed. I slept sound that night, dreaming of the ocean and I woke contented - for the first few minutes anyway.

It was time for me to be free of that prison but I had to do it properly so I would be truly free. The thing that has to be remembered is that the institution believes that patients suffer from an illness that needs medication and treatment to make them well. They have had lot of experience in their field to back up their arguments and the idea that a patient could learn to live and function in society with that condition was alien to them. It seemed the more training and experience they had, the more stubborn in the belief that that they are right they became.

New or fresh members of staff were the easiest to convince as they hadn't been brainwashed or tortured by the institution to believe all patients should be just medicated. They actually listened and offered emotional support. Doctors were the real enemy; they could see through all the games and expected the worst of a patient.

So in short, you are never going get them to agree with your view whether you scream and shout or beg and cry, it would have the same result and most probably end up with you being sedated.

The first rule to remember is if you say you're not sick and don't need medication they will say that's part of your illness and confirm how sick you really are. So you have to make them think you know you're sick and need help. Pretend, pretend, pretend.

Don't you dare say that the medication is killing your mind and leaving you numb, even though it is. It's the same with your inner demon; you can't say you're not ill; it's just an inner voice.

You need to lie; say things like: 'I'm feeling better now I'm on medication' or better still: 'I'm happy to stay in hospital'. Things like that trick them into false sense of security; believe me, I know, I tried it all and it worked. Another thing to remember is; no one gets better without a setback or two. Make an amazing recovery and they will suspect that you are playing them. You need to have a few off-days that get less and less frequent as time goes on. That shows them the treatment is working.

If what you say feels right to them, you are well on your way. But remember; keep the voices to yourself or all your hard work is wasted. I first tried to blame things on my childhood and hardship in my life. I did not mention Catherine or they might have committed me for life. That was just brushed off as a contributing factor of my illness. It wasn't 'til I started saying that I had illness while I was in therapy and was feeling better on the meds that finally the doctors started to ease up on me.

For weeks I got up every day, had breakfast, attended therapies even if I felt like grabbing the staff and ringing their necks. Eventually came the day when the doctors finally set me free.

I stuck on the meds for some time after getting out but they numbed my mind and I hated being on them. Sure they kept her in check, but I just couldn't function on them. Then came the day I finally binned the meds and decided to live free.

It was two days after the meds started to wear off that she came back; quiet at first, then louder and more often. But unlike before, it felt different. Those first few weeks on the outside were hard. I tried to go back home but all who knew me before either felt sorry for me or avoided me like a leper. Was it my fault that I was like that? Was I not the same person they had known all their life?

Friends and family became strangers. Even one of my own brothers distanced himself from me, a fact I could never change. I moved up north, close to the place where my repair had begun, and spent many a day sat on those rocks, looking out to sea, figuring out what I would do with my life and who I was.

A few months later, I travelled back to my home town, where my brother had died and all had turned against me. My friend stuck by me through thick and thin and in time, my past lapsed into history. Very few remember what I am or what happened to me, instead I walk in the shadows. As to my Dark partner, it remains my constant companion and to be honest, I think if it left I'd feel lonely. True, I have to second-guess myself every minute of every day and think more before I act. Also I have to act like a chameleon to fit in but it works. I am not as the doctors said; sick and needing medicating. To be honest, it's a slight personality defect that can be handled.

I did eventually find a woman who could accept me for what I am. She knows I'm not normal and has never asked about my past, but rather, she takes me for what I am. She gave me a son who luckily takes after his mum, not me. He is fifteen now and although his mum and I divorced some years ago, we are the best friends you could imagine.

You're thinking 'why divorced?' That was just a twist of fate and postnatal depression.

# CHAPTER 10

# END GAME

As I sit here alone in the dark with a brandy in my hand, the glow of the fire fills and warms the room. The shadows dance on the walls as the flames of the fire flicker. The smell of old books fills the room from the collection on the shelves. My mind drifts back to a time when I had thought I was alone. Once there was more. Once, there was love. Once there were things that made the heart beat faster.

That was many years ago in a much simpler time 'oh to be that young again'. It was in the 80s when she was unknown to me the Dark passenger that shares my mind and soul.

She was the one, and many times over the years we have sat and remembered the first time we spoke. Looking out of the window, the snow's falling harder, like a white blanket covering the land. Looking out of my windows I see all those people trying to escape the blizzards. Each one seems so alone, so cold in their own shell, fighting step by step to find their way home. If I could feel sympathy, I would; they are the ones they call 'normal' - alone in their empty shells.

Sure, mine and my Dark passenger's journey to understanding and unison may have been hard and long as you have gathered from all you have read here.

For many years, I might have fought to be free of her or to control her and failed, almost meeting my own destruction once or twice. It was not easy; my own self-doubts about not being good enough weighed heavy on me.

So how do you control your inner demon? It starts with becoming aware of him or her. Start becoming aware of the responses what are yours and what's triggered by the inner demon. Start noticing your emotional response and try to put it into words. Why do you feel that way? What logic is your mind using to justify the emotion? Challenge it. Most of the time, if we dig deep enough, we can see that our fear, anger, anxiety, and even depression is unjustified and blown out of proportion.

I had nearly wrecked things before we started to learn and accept each other.

As I put a fresh log on the fire, she cries and in my mind the thought, 'if only she was happy and I would never be alone'. She will guard me from and stop me being lost to the darkness of eternity.

Together we have shared so much; life, death and possibly what is held between. She who feels she must be obeyed. The darkness that sits inside my mind, my relationship with her had started to change. When she first appeared, I wanted shot of her and her insults and complaints, but as time went on, she has become less critical and might even be becoming - I know it's weird - a kind of friend. Though I still didn't trust her and her advice - if I did, the body count would be high. I have lost count of the amount of times I heard her say deep inside the recesses of my mind:

'Do they really have to live?'

The other favourite is: 'You'd be doing them a favour.'

She was, and is, an ardent supporter of final justice. I sometimes ask myself if she is part of me and is she just saying what I really want? I realise that was a dangerous path to walk and I removed all such thoughts from my head.

She is my Darkness and something I rarely allow into this world, as every time she came out, I knew blood or misery would follow. The few times she did get loose, I was told those around could see in my eyes it wasn't me and the strength and violence that followed was on another level.

Long into the night, as we sit and watch inside our mind, figures appear out of the darkness, bent on destruction and all types of horrors. Families hold hands, praying for deliverance, beings moving past us like ghosts in the night. Dark worlds that only we can see; this is the gift we share together as we now put these words on paper for all to read.

The dream we once had and the darkness we overcame while laid in that hospital bed has brought us into a new world and together we share our stories with the world.

Being aware of the irrational thoughts and fears is the first and most crucial step to getting rid of them and taming the inner darkness. Trying to just fight what's inside is part of a losing battle. If I had known that in the early days, most of the pain and hardship I endured would not have been necessary.

Though a lot of what I went through, like Paris and my friends in the Asylum, I am glad of. Yes, I know I call them friends, even though my kind can count few as friends.

Now comes the kicker - early in my story, I told you I do everything for a reason; that this book was written for a reason.

The reason is my books are an extension of the darkness I hold deep inside and the journeys we take together in the recesses of my mind travelling through life and our dreams. To fully understand and enjoy them, it was fitting that you read how it all began.

Each story we write will go deeper and darker, venturing into this dark world. So if this book disturbed you in any way, get out now, while you can. Because the true horrors are due to begin.

**In the next book, she's not going to allow me to be so nice...**

# ABOUT THE AUTHOR

Jason was born in Reading, Berkshire at the beginning of May 1972. As the second-born of six children, Due to the Death of his older Brother Jason spent his early adult years traveling and exploring the world around him.

In recent times due to illness and disability, he had been forced to restructure his career path. No longer able to follow his existing career as an Information system Consultant, he decided to embark on a new challenge.

From a childhood age, he loved books and dreamed of being able to write them. With the aid of the Open University and there disability department this dream has become a reality

www.ingramcontent.com/pod-product-compliance
Ingram Content Group UK Ltd.
Pitfield, Milton Keynes, MK11 3LW, UK
UKHW020223250726
13967UKWH00001B/167